"*The Cleansing* will bear mentioning in the same breath with Lovecraft and Robert Bloch and Robert E. Howard, with as compelling a voice as any such Architects of the Weird."

— MICHAEL H. PRICE, AUTHOR OF
THE *FORGOTTEN HORRORS* BOOK SERIES

"So original and so scary . . . It will be a long time before I sleep as soundly as I did before *Old Fears* . . . A rare and chilling treat."

—WHITLEY STREIBER, AUTHOR OF *THE HUNGER*

"*Old Fears* is a psychological thriller of unusual power . . . I locked the door while reading it."

— DARCY O'BRIEN, EDGAR AWARD-WINNING AUTHOR OF *POWER TO HURT*

" . . . a modern masterpiece."

— C. DEAN ANDERSSON, AUTHOR OF
THE BLOODSONG SAGA (FOR *OLD FEARS*)

" . . . the quintessential horror story."

— *THE DAYTON DAILY NEWS* (FOR *OLD FEARS*)

BEAUTY AND THE BUND

BEAUTY AND THE BUND

DEMONS IN D.C.
BOOK ONE

ROBERT A. BROWN

JOHN WOOLEY

eBook ISBN: 978-1-964832-27-2

Paperback ISBN: 978-1-964832-28-9

First edition by Babylon Books

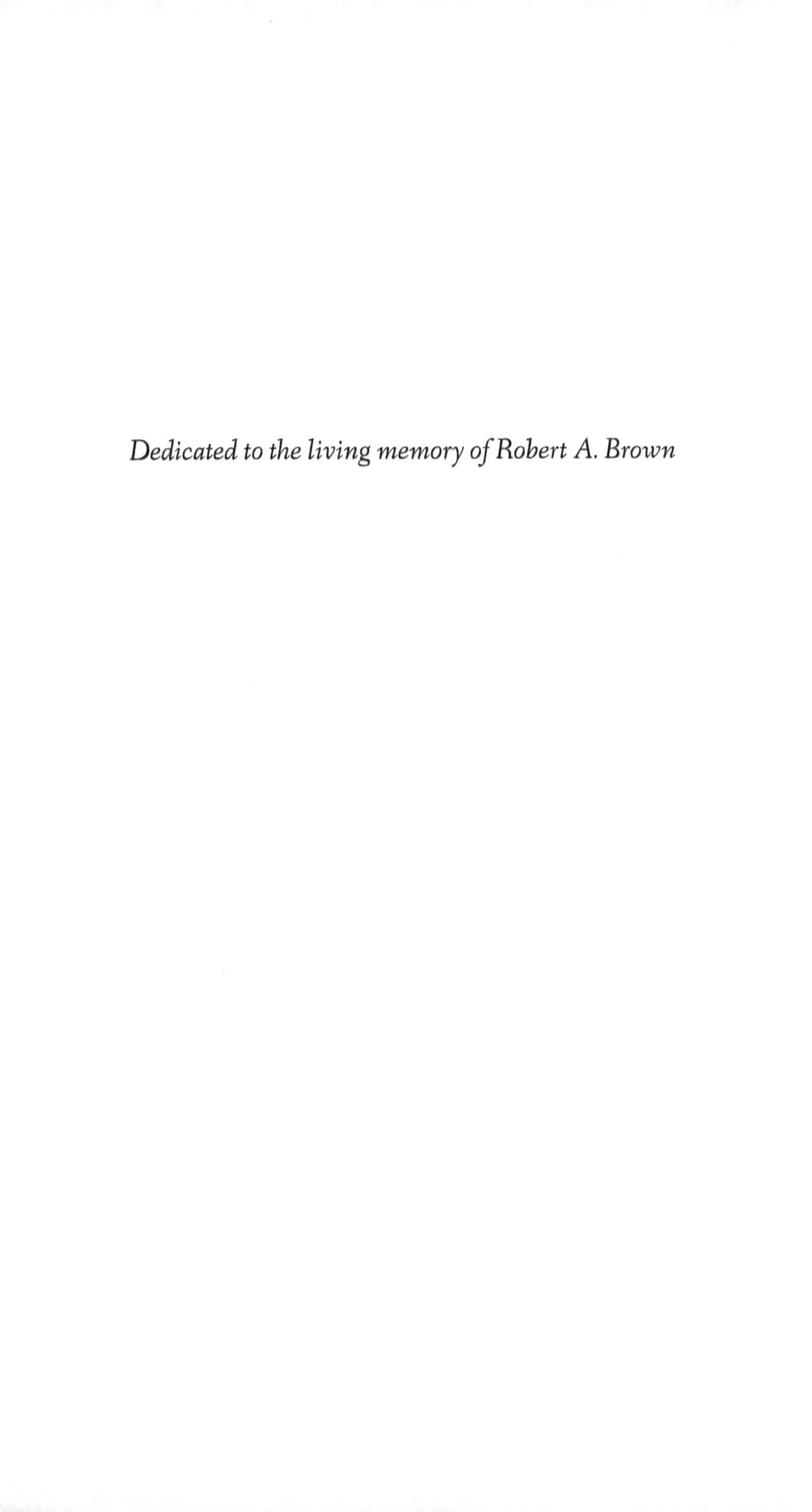

Dedicated to the living memory of Robert A. Brown

September 30, 1939
Saturday (Hooray!)

Dear John,

   Yep, it's been an entire week since I
rolled a sheet into this trusty old typer and
knocked out a message to you. I guess maybe I
should apologize, but then again, maybe I
shouldn't, because believe me, pal, this week
has been more like, as the cliché goes, a
month of Sundays. In fact, there's been so
damned much going on that I get weary just
thinking about how long it's going to take to
tell you about everything that's happened to
your faithful correspondent.

   But I'm going to. It may take me two or
three runs at it, and it'll maybe even get
stretched over a couple of days, but you'll
get the whole megillah, even if it's in parts
you'll have to assemble like a jigsaw puzzle.

   If this all sounds a little detached or
strange, well, it's because that's exactly
the way I've been feeling ever since I hit
"the City of Magnificent Intentions," as our
friend Charles Dickens called it. I know I
sent you a chipper little missive last Sunday
about how damned lovely everything was here:
the friendly hackie who dropped me off at my
new workplace, the clean apartment they'd set
me up in, full to overflowing with happy boys

and girls, so peppy that I half-expected some of them to suddenly start dancing and singing in the lobby, like I'd suddenly taken up residence in a Metro-Goldwyn-Mayer musical.

That was before I found out that a few too many of those boys favored brown shirts.

I don't mean they were Nazi assault troopers, of course. As far as I know, those brown shirts are still over in Germany attending to the needs of Brother Adolph, while he's busy invading Poland and challenging the rest of Europe. I'm talking instead about members of the German-American Bund, that group that's supposed to be telling the rest of us how much Germany loves the U.S.A., etc., etc. Remember that big to-do they had at Madison Square Garden back on Washington's Birthday? A "pro-America rally" for "True Americanism" — that's how they ballyhooed it. The photos were in all the papers. I'll bet your very own Saint Paul Dispatch ran a few of 'em. There was that huge vertical banner of George Washington behind the podium, surrounded by equally big banners of the Stars and Stripes, alternating with flags that (if I remember right) represented the Bund — a big swastika in the middle, coming out at you from an Iron Cross. It seemed kind of nutty to me then — still does — putting the Father of Our Country and Nazis together in the same place, and I guess it seemed that way to a lot of other people, too, because there were plenty of protests that night.

Their leader, Fritz Kuhn, has gotten in plenty of hot water for dipping into the Bund till to line his own pockets (and, as I understand it, to shower on his girlfriends). He did it so much and so often that he spent some time up there in the New York City Tombs; he may be out now. Winchell writes a lot about him in his column, and what he says ain't pretty.

Hell, I'm sure you know a whole lot more about this than I do, now that I think about it. You're the guy who works for a newspaper.

Anyway, as it turns out, one of Kuhn's followers is my next-door neighbor. And, get this: He's got a Brooklyn accent, which plays hell with the patois of the Fatherland.

Let me digress:

Having a goose-stepper right next to me is just one of the reasons this apartment building isn't nearly as swell as I wrote earlier. In fact, it's a dump. I don't even have a window, for cat's sake. And I guess this is as good a time as any to tell you that after I pounded my ear for most of last Saturday and Sunday, which seems like a million years ago, I've had trouble sleeping in this forsaken place. I'm starting to get some good shots of the blues from these bare walls and worn-out carpet, with the single wooden rail chair, rickety desk, and the chest of drawers that apparently came over on the Mayflower representing the only sticks of furniture besides my bed — which is comfortable enough, I guess, but not exactly what you'd find at the Ritz. I keep waking up in the night like an old man and feeling like I imagine old men feel when they wake up in the night.

My sleeplessness surely has something to do with Elrich — and if that's his real name, I'll eat my newsboy cap — the homegrown Nazi boy I just met, who seems to have his Hun chums over every night to listen to German oompah music on the Victrola and, hell, drink beer and eat wiener schnitzel, for all _I_ know. They get a little loud some nights, but after sleeping in CCC camps as long as I did, something like that shouldn't bother me.

It's more — well, to be honest, I think it has more to do with the seventh sense. I haven't felt it _every_ night since I moved in, but when I do, there's no mistaking what it is. Something's going on right past the wall next to my bed, and whatever it is, it's not just a man-made menace.

I realize what you may be thinking. Here I am, in a new place surrounded by new people, my . . . _experiences_ in Arkansas still fresh in my mind, so quite naturally I'm going to have the quivering pips for a few days. You're figuring maybe what I'm calling the seventh sense isn't really that at all this time; it's just an unease about my surroundings and a hangover from everything that happened to me in my final days and nights back in the middle of the country.

Well, sure, I've thought about that. And I've thought that maybe having a bunch of goose-steppers congregating next door to me every night might have something to do with my jitters as well. But I know these little fascist muttonheads aren't anything to worry about — especially since their big daddy Adolph decided to start the war in Europe. These guys never were exactly beloved by their fellow citizens, and now that their leader's invaded Poland, you know that the average Joe on the street has turned even more against them.

Again, though, I'm confident the Bund isn't what's causing my seventh sense to tingle. It's something else; something — well, maybe something that's not human at all. I don't know what it is yet, but I do know it has something to do with Elrich and his chums.

Now, some more about that neighbor of mine. He's a young guy, big and tough-looking, muscular enough but already going to fat, who gives you one of those soft, moist handshakes. And he's gung-ho for the Bund. A homegrown Kraut, of course, but, he claims, a true American. He first broached me Tuesday or Wednesday evening, I can't remember which, after I'd gotten back here from work, still trying to figure out all that was going on in my new life and wondering who might be having all that nighttime revelry next door to me. I had my key in the lock when he emerged from his room. When he saw me, he grinned like a possum eating wasps and stuck out his pudgy hand. He straightened up a little too, taking on what he must've figured was a military bearing. I think it was because he wanted me to notice his getup. I think I told you these guys were brown shirts, but I meant it metaphorically. On this night, the first time I'd seen him in his club regalia, he had on a white shirt and black trousers and held onto a black garrison cap — those flat cloth caps known informally (for some reason or other) as "piss cutters."

"Hey dere, _mein freund_," he said, Brooklyn accent clashing with German like a polka-dotted bow tie with a striped shirt. "I'm Elrich, yah neighbor. New in da city, yah?"

I told him I was, gave him my name, and shook hands. It was like gripping a tuna. A few others started piling out of the doorway then, all dressed exactly like him. A couple had their caps atop their heads, and on one side I could see that symbol from the flags in the Madison Square Garden photos — the three-dimensional swastika atop a red Iron Cross. They looked me up and down, not exactly hostile, but a little wary. Again, they've got to know that more and more of their neighbors are seeing Hitler for what he is, and for what _they_ are for following him, so I imagine all of 'em are a bit edgier than normal these days.

"We're German-American Bund. One hundred

percent Americans!" Elrich pronounced as I was getting the once-over from his chums. "Gotta meeting tonight. Join us, ja?"

I managed a smile. "No, thanks. I'm beat. Maybe some other time."

At that point, a man came out behind the rest of them, dressed in what looked like an expensive suit. He was older and bigger than the rest, his features more straightforwardly German and a little lupine, and when his eyes hit mine, I felt a small unexpected extrasensory jolt. Our eyes locked for a moment, but the contact was broken when the still-grinning Elrich reached into an inside pocket, produced a pamphlet, and pressed it into my hand.

"Ja," he said. "Dis'll tell you about us, pally, and you can find headquarters from what's printed here on dis sheet. C'm'on next week, mein freund. Hear da songs and speaker. You'll like it."

I nodded as I watched them take off down the hall, self-consciously striding, holding themselves erect, the big older one following silently, like a wolf stalking prey. Then I looked at the small flyer in my hand. It was in four colors and professionally produced, promoting America and Americanism while denouncing the "Zionist conspiracy" and "Jew-controlled newspapers" that had put their founder, Kuhn, behind bars. Seeing the name of our President intentionally spelled

"Rosenfelt" was the last straw. I crumpled the flyer up.

After a moment's thought, though, I smoothed it back out. If the seventh sense was telling me something about this bunch, I figured I'd better listen. And the best way to listen, maybe, would be to go to one of those meetings myself to see what gives.

I haven't done it yet, but I plan to whenever the next one comes along, which I'll bet will be soon. Meanwhile, every time I'm about to go to sleep and I have one of those seventh-sense twitches while I'm listening to their muffled talk and music from next door, I tell myself that playing along with these goose-steppers may get me into some trouble, but it's damn sure the right thing to do.

I'll tell you about the rest of my first week in the American Rome later. Maybe I'll even include that second letter in the same envelope with this one. But right now, the past few days have caught up with me, and I'm fighting with myself about a mid-afternoon nap.

I don't really want to take one — I'd like to keep writing this letter instead. But I think that's a battle I'm going to lose.

Your pal and faithful correspondent,
   Robert

September 30, 1939 (continued)
Saturday evening

Dear John,

Well, the arms of Morpheus got me in a wrestler's headlock and wouldn't let go. I kept trying to rouse myself after napping for an hour or so, but it was no good. I just now looked at the clock. Eight fifteen! Holy moley! I've been checked out for nearly six hours!

Guess my first week of work wore me out more than I thought.

Now, though, I'm fully back in the land of the living, and I figure this would be as good a time as any to let you know a little more about the past few days. You know that I'm out of the habit of keeping carbons of my letters to you; I quit that when I got suspicious of some of the folks back in Arkansas, worrying that they might case my room while I was gone and find out more than I wanted 'em to know. The reason I mention this is because I can't remember exactly what and how much I wrote you last week, when I was fresh off the train and still sizing things up here.

For instance, I can't remember if I told you that someone had somehow slipped an envelope into one of my bags before I left Mackaville, and I didn't even know about it until I'd gotten to this place and unpacked. Now that I think about it, I'll bet I <u>didn't</u> tell you about it yet, because it was stuck between my undershirts and I'd just pulled 'em out in a stack and shoved them in my chest of drawers once I got here.So I didn't find the envelope until a few days ago.

John, it was full of money. Hundred-dollar bills, more than I've ever seen at one time. There were twenty of those bills in that one fat envelope, along with a short note that read, "Remember us. But please — never tell." It wasn't signed, but I figure Miss Mary Lou Castle was the only one in town who could afford to let go of that kind of cabbage.

Five words and 2,000 dollars. Four hundred dollars for every word. That's a hell of a ratio, isn't it? I know you're happy to get a penny a word for your pulp stories. I would be, too.

But you know, once I got over the shock of seeing all that geetus, I realized that it would provide me with the means to take up residence somewhere other than this Nazi-infested dump and my windowless cell. Sure, the government set me up here, but I checked with my supervisor, Mr. Fletcher, and he said there's no particular rule against moving somewhere else, if you can find a place. The way he said it, though, with kind of a Franklin Pangborn sniff, made it clear he thought I was being difficult. I can't say his attitude bothered me very much, but I don't want to get an early reputation as a malcontent, either. First impressions are hard to shake.

Anyway, I'm going to see about maybe finding a rooming house, like I had back in Arkansas. I don't expect lightning to strike twice — to find another Ma Stean or anything like that. But I just plain don't like it here. It took only a few days for the miserableness of the place to seep into my bones. Having a Nazi next door doesn't help things, either.

I don't think my discontent has anything to do with the seventh sense, or the unease I've felt run through me sometimes when the big fellow and his Bund chums get together at night. This apartment house just isn't any good. It's that simple.

Well, enough about poor me and my sad, sad life. I'll admit, as I may have written you earlier, that this room and this bed looked pretty good to me after that long train trip without the luxury of a sleeper. Looking back on it, not getting one was kind of stupid of me. Over the two days and one night I was aboard, I probably gave enough away to the porters to have paid for an upper berth, with cash left over. And if I'd known about that pile in Miss Castle's envelope — well, no sense crying over spilt milk. Like we used to say, it just makes it salty for the cat.

Really, I guess, it wasn't all that bad. I was so relieved to shake the Mackaville dust off my feet that I was able to catch several hours of sleep sitting up, no matter how loud or rough the ride got. The regular clacking of the wheels and the soft nighttime voices of the surrounding riders lulled me. I had a window seat, too, and when I was jolted awake or woke up for some other reason, I'd turn my head and watch the stars and the lights of the little towns as we sped along, and soon I'd be out again.

As you know, I'm a traditionalist when it comes to trains, and I sure would've preferred a big steam engine instead of the diesel I got, but to leave Mackaville I'd have taken a government mule and ridden him bareback through barbed wire.

I said something about the porters a couple of paragraphs ago. Whenever one of them did something for me, I made a point of asking his name instead of calling him "George," like so many white people do. Every one of them seemed to appreciate that, as well as the tips I gave for any service rendered. I detest that tradition of dime tips, so my usual was a fifty-cent piece. I started the trip with a whole pocketful, but I gave so many away that I had to buy a couple more rolls along the way. My favorite porter, whose name was Chris, happily took care of that transaction for me, knowing that a good share of 'em would probably end up with him.

I have no idea where he got the rolls of

half bucks, although I have a better idea where he and another porter, Adam, got the three miniature bottles of Crown Royal they brought me when I was having my dinner the first day of the trip. They smuggled it right to my table, hidden in a rolled-up newspaper, both of them grinning. I know they sell miniature bottles of booze like that when the trains go through "wet" states, and these even came in tiny velvet bags.

I knew then why James had casually asked me a little earlier if I "ever enjoyed a nice drink with dinner." It had puzzled me at the time, since I didn't think I'd be able to buy any booze on the train, what with the tangle of "dry" counties in Arkansas, Tennessee, and Virginia we had to pass through. But I'd told him that I was partial to a good Canadian whisky like Crown Royal. (Despite the best efforts of certain members of the Mackaville citizenry, my enthusiasm for corn squeezins remains low.)

When I spied the familiar-looking little bags hidden inside the newspaper, I smiled my thanks and reached into my pocket, only to have Chris say, "Nossir. This one's on us. We like to see our friends have a good time."

"Enjoy that nice steak," added Adam with a big wink. And I did.

I think I've written you about most of the rest of it. I had Chris wake me up at four in the morning, because I wanted to get into the men's room and shower and shave before the usual crush came through.So I shucked the civilian clothes I'd been wearing and put on a fresh starched khaki shirt with military pleats, a black tie, and clean starched jodhpurs. I'd spent some time polishing my military dress shoes and leather leggings, and when I put everything on and checked myself out in the mirror, I thought I looked pretty good. (You remember that an officer's uniform is just about the only CCC-issued clothing that has any style; everything else shouts "down on the farm."So busting my tail to make lieutenant back then has turned out to pay dividends years down the line. When I wore that outfit, people on the train figured I was regular military, and I admit I didn't do anything to disabuse them of that notion.)

At seven a.m., I hit the dining car and ordered up melon, eggs, grits, a double rasher of bacon, and a tall glass of milk with ice in it. This did me up fine. (The coffee on the train was too strong for my taste.) After that, I headed to the observation car, which didn't have anyone in it at that hour, set up the typer, and started writing the letter you got, I'm assuming, last week. As I finished the missive, I fired up one of the two Bering cigars I'd put in the inside pocket of my uniform. You know my weakness for those particular stogies, even though they're a bit of an extravagance. I hadn't been able to find any in Mackaville, but I'd managed to lay in a few of 'em from a tobacco counter at one of our train stops.

Just about that time, a little bald, blintz-shaped Jewish man, immaculately dressed, entered the car. He nodded at me, and since it was only the two of us, I felt it only fair to ask if the smoke was going to bother him.

He grinned. "Oh, my, no," he said, sniffing at the smoke. "I'm a cigar connoisseur myself. That's a Bering, isn't it?"

That hit me as funny. Maybe he really did know the smell of a Bering, or the look of one, or maybe he'd spotted the trademark glass tube it had come in, which now sat empty beside me. But there was joy on his face, and before I'd really thought about it, I had the other glass-encased cigar out and was leaning forward, offering it to him.

"Well, I'm not Professor Quiz," I said, "so you don't get a cash prize for being right. But I can offer you this nice fresh Bering."

"Oh, goodness no. I couldn't," he said, looking from me to the cigar and back to me again.

"Sure you could," I returned. "You're obviously a gentleman of taste, and I always enjoy it more when I'm smoking with someone else." I shook the tube a little. "Please. From one lonely traveler to another."

Indecision played across his face, but I didn't need my seventh sense to know how this was going to come out. Before he reached for the Bering, however, his eyes met mine and he said, "I will accept your offer with grati-tude — but only if you will come to my store when you reach D.C. and allow me to sell you something at a discount. You <u>are</u> going to our nation's capitol, yes? I deduced that from your uniform."

I said he was right.

"Then you will visit me."

"Sure."

Now John, I don't want to generalize, but it's been my experience, limited though it may be, that people of Mr. Gold's race never like to accept something — even something as small as a nice cigar — without offering a favor in return. As he worked a business card out of his waistcoat and handed it to me, I saw that his name was Hyrum Gold and that he owned a haber-dashery called "Hy's Fine Clothes for Men." I got a little thrill when I thought of how fate had once again worked for me. I knew one of the first things I was going to have to do when I hit town was buy some dress clothes to go with the three changes I'd brought along. (Of course, I couldn't wear my CCC duds to a job with the military. For one thing, it'd create too much confusion.) Now, I knew where I would go to get that little chore accomplished.

I nodded my thanks and passed him the glass tube containing the Bering, along with my little silver alligator cigar clipper. He sniffed delicately as he opened the tube and then, carefully, used the cutter to make a hole at the business end of the stogie. Soon, two happy cigar lovers were busy filling the air of the observation car with rich, aromatic smoke, and Mr. Gold was telling me all about how much the city of Washington had changed since he'd opened up his place. We talked for several minutes, puffing contentedly away, until a couple of older ladies came in, wrinkling up their noses at the smell of our cigars and looking daggers at us.

I checked my strap watch and saw that we were getting close to our destination.So with a wink at Mr. Gold, I shut up my typer's case and, with the Bering still in my mouth, left the observation car.

He didn't follow. But I knew I'd be seeing him again soon.

I guess that's about for catching you up, except for a few things about the job. It's certainly not the most exciting employment I've ever had, especially after Maokaville. Basically, I sit and type orders — supply orders, movement orders, promotion orders, etc. — for the Army. I start my days with about 50 and it's a Sisyphean task, because as soon as I get a few done, Fletcher piles a few more on my desk. He's not really a bad guy — a little on the fussy side, as I noted earlier, and his breath could use a few regular doses of Sen-Sen — but I don't have any real problems with him.

I do have problems, though, with the cafeteria food here. It's sort of tasteless and I think it smells a little funny, like a lot of institutional food, so I've been getting a couple of bottles of Coca-Cola out of the soft-drink machine on our floor and making those my lunch. The good thing about that is I can work at my desk throughout the half-hour lunch period while I sip the Cokes, so I get quite a bit more done than the other clerks. Although I don't know if Mr. Fletcher is quite sure what to make of me yet — whether I'm going to be more go-getter or troublemaker — he sure seems to like the fact that I'm taking care of so much work every day. I sometimes even stay late, leaving after everyone else, including him, has gone home.

I won't tell him that the reason has less to do with me trying to apple-polish than it does with my growing antipathy toward my own "home." I just don't want to go back to that dreary place until I absolutely have to.

And now, I've got the Bund to consider, and the seventh-sense warning that seems to be triggered by that bunch on an all-too-regular basis. Their next meeting is Wednesday, and I've made up my mind to go just to see what it's all about, so the next time you hear from me I will have been there and you'll get a full report.

Don't think I can go back to sleep yet, even though it's quiet next door. Luckily, I've found a good second-hand bookstore that's got stacks of pulps, and I was able to snag three of the <u>Operator No. 5</u> issues from earlier this year for a jitney each. So I'm planning on spending a good hour or two catching up with the Yellow Vulture, his Oriental menaces, and their invasion of America — and trying not to think that it could possibly come true in this crazy age.

Your pal and faithful correspondent,
Robert

October 5, 1939
Thursday evening

Dear John,

Well, I made the Bund meeting, all right.
It was last night, and as I took it in, I
kept thinking about the detailed description
I was going to write you when I got back
here. I wanted especially to get across how
much it seemed to me like a lot of potentially dangerous foolishness.

But then, as W.C. Fields said in <u>Man on
the Flying Trapeze,</u> things happened.

After work yesterday, I came back, show-
ered, and changed into my CCC uniform. I
briefly considered taking along the old Colt
.45, that cavalry pistol the Black brothers
gave me back in Mackaville, but it was so big
that I couldn't have concealed it on my
person; I would've had to carry it in a
briefcase. And if this happened to be the
kind of clambake that required its attendees
to be patted down at the door, I would've not
only had a hard time explaining why I'd
brought it, but I also might not have gotten
it back without some effort.

I decided on the CCC uniform because it
looked military, and might impress, or intim-
idate, or both, the young goose-steppers I
was going to be around. If they really were

"One hundred percent American," like Elrich had told me, in his Heinie Brooklynese, then I figured they'd consider having an American military man in their midst something to be proud about.

I'd just finished dressing when I got the knock on my door. When I opened it, I saw about a half dozen young guys, Elrich in front, all spiffed up in those black-and-white outfits with the red symbols on their caps. Maybe it was my imagination, but they seemed to take a pretty good interest in my uniform.

"Ah, _mein freund_, you're ready to go," he beamed. "I'm tellin' you, you're gonna lap this up, _ja_?"

I nodded and followed them to the elevator, where I couldn't help but notice how the wizened old operator wrinkled up his nose when we piled in. I'd been chewing the fat with him a little bit since I'd moved into the place, but when he saw I was with those guys, he wouldn't even look at me.

Like I wrote you earlier, the tide seems to really be turning against the whole idea of the German-American Bund. I got another example of that when we left the apartment building and caught the attention of a gaggle of pool-hall types who were hanging around a corner about a half-block away. They started yelling catcalls at us, using terms like "goose-steppers," krauts," and "jerries" — and those were the kinder ones. Figuring this might be the prelude to a melee, I shot a glance at Elrich.

"Pay no attention to those <u>shiza kopfs</u>, pally," Elrich said to me, stiffening his shoulders even more. I kept an eye on 'em anyway, even though my seventh sense was quiet as a churchyard mouse, and when we walked down the sidewalk away from them they kept hollering for a while but didn't follow. In a few minutes, we'd caught a trolley, which deposited us after a short ride in what I instantly saw was a classier part of town.

I followed the junior Nazis to a dark storefront which had "Zander Jewelry" taste-fully emblazoned on its display window in red and gold lettering. We weren't there long before the door clicked open and we passed through in single file, slipping by an indis-tinct figure standing in the shadows of the interior, beside the door. We went by several display cases, and I could tell, even in the darkness, that this place housed some pretty expensive sparklers.

I noticed something else, too. My seventh sense was starting to rev up. At first, I thought it might have been triggered by that shadowy character who'd let us in. As we left him behind and went down some stairs under a trap door into the store's basement, though, my warning system stayed at the same level. Even though it wasn't growing any stronger, I reminded myself to be extra wary, just in case.

The surroundings were spartan, but warm and reasonably well-lit, with maybe a couple dozen more Bund members, all in their regalia, gathered around a table that held bottles of soda and cookies and chatting away. Except for the swastikas, it could've been a Presbyterian Church youth social back in Minnesota. But those weird little flags with the telescoped swastikas were planted all around the place and hanging from the walls, often next to American flags — like at Madison Square Garden, only on a much smaller scale, and without any banner of George Washington. At the end of the hall was a small stage with a lectern, which had several rows of folding chairs facing it.

And you know what, John? There were women there. A trio of 'em. Nice-looking, too, in their twenties or maybe early thirties, all three dressed in white blouses and black skirts, the same color scheme as their male counterparts. Seeing them gave me a bit of a shock. I don't know why I expected to see all men at this wingding — maybe it was because I figured the guys in the Bund were pretty <u>declasse</u>, if you get what I mean — not the high-roller types or street-corner Lotharios who'd attract these kinds of tomatoes. Plus, now that I think about it, I couldn't imagine young women of this caliber falling for Uncle Adolph's Nazi crap. It just wasn't right.

That seventh sense was still buzzing as I walked up to the table and opened a nice cold bottle of Delaware Punch. Mixed in with the sweaty odor of the Bund boys, I caught the unmistakable flowery smell of Shalimar perfume. You remember our hotcha speech teacher back in Hallock, Miss Lake? Of course you do. I don't know which one of us had the bigger crush on her. But once I got up the courage to ask her what kind of perfume she used, and she told me "Shalimar," enunciating in that perfect English she always tried to use, I've been able to recognize it ever since.

My hosts were falling all over themselves to try and entertain these young women, going on about the Bund and Americanism and their "cause," sometimes spitting cookie crumbs in the air as they tried to talk above one another. Grabbing me by the arm, Elrich introduced me to the three girls, looking pleased with himself about bringing in the new guy. I remember that one of this covey, an Italian beauty built like a brick outhouse, was named Karen something, and another was a Mrs. Green, who was apparently married to one of the Bund boys.

And the third one? _Mamma mia!_ Her name was Gena Laubauch (I'm spelling the last name like it sounds) and she was five feet and six inches of gorgeous face and figure. I immediately sized her up as the hot number of this bunch, and she damn sure knew it. I could see it in the sultry way her blue eyes narrowed when Elrich did the honors.

"Ah, Mr. Brown," she said, holding out her hand, which I took. Hell, I wanted to kiss it like Maurice Chevalier or somebody, but I restrained myself. "I'm so glad to see a new face around here — and a real soldier, too."

The way she said "real" seemed to me to be an obvious reference to the pretend Nazis that were panting all around her.

"I hate to disillusion you, Miss Laubauch," I said, letting go of a hand that clung to mine for just an extra second or two. "But this is the uniform of the Civilian Conservation Corps. I've had it for some time now."

She smiled, cat-like, showing a row of remarkably white and even teeth.

"You admit it," she said. "I like that."

"You knew?"

"Oh, yes." She tossed her blonde curls. "My brother is in the CCC. But at least the uniform you're wearing was issued to you — you didn't have to <u>pay</u> for it."

Sweeping her arm, she indicated the Bund boys around her, who looked away with embarrassment.

"Well hell — 'scuse me, <u>fraulein</u> — you know we get orders from th' top about exactly what we have to wear, and it ain't cheap to keep up," Elrich said. "Seems like half my paycheck goes for uniforms, and membership cards, and badges and stuff like that there. It's O.K., though. Shows our dedication to the cause, ja?"

She smiled, cat-like. "And what did you have to give for <u>your</u> uniform, Mr. Brown?" she asked.

I grinned back at her. "Oh, about two years of my life."

"Indeed. And I suppose I shouldn't be so critical of my <u>kamerads</u>. As you can see, we ladies have our own dress code." At that point, she took a deep breath, just so I could see how well her blouse fit. And it fit very well indeed, like a white cellophane wrapper over a pair of bon bons.

As I took in the sights, the sense of danger that had been humming through me suddenly jumped like the needle on a seismograph. Looking up, I saw someone descending the stairs — the same hard-eyed older German man who'd been next door to me a few days ago. Like then, he was in civilian clothes, and while I can't swear it, I think Gena flinched when he left the stairway and started toward us.

I couldn't blame her, John. My seventh sense was roaring through me like an air-raid siren as he approached. He was looking at me, not her, staring me down through half-lidded eyes — and I swear to God, as I watched they began glowing green! I'd never seen that in a person before. Emerald-green, almost transparent, and sending wave after wave of pure hatred at me. As our eyes locked, the green glow in his irises changed to a regular, darker hue, but the hate still flowed. I

could feel it burning through my whole body —
and with it, a strong animalistic sense, as
though I were staring into the eyes of a
feral beast — a wolf. I could almost smell
the wildness.

The whole thing only lasted a few seconds
— maybe less. Then, he turned away, toward
Gena. With hammering insides, I watched as
she went to him, the others around her quiet
and still, and they embraced. He kissed her,
hard, and then over her shoulder, he looked
at me again. And for just a moment, the eyes
pulsed green.

Then, he grinned. Or maybe it was more of
a smirk, as he crushed Gena against his own
body.

Of course, there's more. A hell of a lot
more.

As the marquee outside the Maribel Theatre
used to say, it's "coming soon."

Your pal and faithful correspondent,
Robert

October 6, 1939
<u>early</u> Friday morning

Dear John,

There's so much more to tell that I've had a hard time sleeping. In fact, I haven't grabbed but three or four hours of shut-eye. So here I am again, banging away at my Remington, wondering about what's going on next door, even though I haven't heard a peep from that direction, and knowing that I've got to get out of this place, and in jig time.

So, then. The meeting.

Following that tete-a-tete with Gena and her boyfriend — Elrich took me aside right afterwards and told me his name was Fehring (I had him spell it) and he was "the real thing," whatever the hell that might mean — the whole shebang got started. One of the white-shirted Bund guys took the stage with plenty of pumped-up self-importance and told everybody to be seated. The 20 or 30 people gathered there in the basement traipsed over to the folding chairs, with Fehring and Gena heading right for the front row, and I hung back, standing in the shadows behind the last line of chairs, thinking about what I'd seen in the man's eyes and trying to get my seventh sense to settle down a little.

Behind me, a door opened in the back wall, and a squat little guy sporting a toothbrush mustache that was a rank copy of <u>der Fuhrer's</u> came out, with a uniformed man on either side of him. But his two bodyguards weren't cut from the same cloth as the rank-and-file members — or, at least, their clothing wasn't. Their shirts <u>were</u> brown — no metaphor this time. They wore the same sort of black pants as the run-of-the-mill Bundists, the same garrison caps with the red symbol, but each one sported a Sam Browne belt, with that strap over the right shoulder. Both of them also had blackjacks stuck in the belts around their waists.

The idea seemed to be for them to look plenty tough, and they succeeded.

Condescendingly scanning the crowd as they walked their little charge down the center aisle, they escorted him up to the stage and then stood in front of it, one on either side, while he took three steps up to stand beside the lectern as a skinny, pimply-faced young Bundist gave him a flowery introduction. The kid went on for a while about how this shrimp was a big cheese (excuse the mixed metaphor) in the eastern <u>gau</u>, which I think was their term for a regional Bund outfit, and then the little guy bowed and stepped to the microphone.

A small phonograph had been set up, right on the lip of the stage, and he reached down and put the needle on the record. Out came an instrumental version of "The Star-Spangled Banner." Everyone stood then, and lustily sang our National Anthem, with the pint-sized speaker waving his arms in the air like Stowkowski.

Watching and listening to them, I had the thought flash through my mind that, well, maybe these Bundists aren't such bad sorts after all. And then, the guy put another record on. And when _that_ music started, every arm in the place (except mine) shot up in that sieg-heil Nazi salute. The little guy gave it right back to 'em, and then they all started singing again. If their rendition of "The Star-Spangled Banner" had been lusty, the treatment they gave this one was even more full-throated. Unfortunately, it all was in German, so I can't tell you what it was about. I think I've heard the tune before, though, maybe in a newsreel report about Nazi Germany.

I'm pretty sure I didn't hear it on _Your Hit Parade_.

At the end, the guy at the podium shouted, "Free America!" And the crowd seig-heiled right back at him, repeating his two words.

If I hadn't known by then how misguided I was to think these dunderheads might be O.K. after all, it would only have taken a couple of minutes of this crumb's speech to convince me forever.

John, I'm not going to go into much detail about what this little Nazi said from the stage in his Germanic accent, except to tell you that it was all a double load of crap, lies told for truth. He started out talking about how their "beloved Fritz Kuhn" had been thrown unjustly into prison in New York for a crime that was purely made up by the government. Apparently, a few days earlier, the district attorney had raised the amount of Kuhn's bail from $5,000 to $50,000, and when he couldn't pay it, they'd jugged him in the Tombs.

And whose fault was this? Kuhn's, for embezzling money from the Bund treasury?

Oh, hell no. It was the Jews.

They controlled the newspapers, and they controlled the courts, and poor little Fritz Kuhn hadn't had a chance.

I'd been ready for him to excoriate Jews, since that's the party line, but I was unprepared for just how vile and vitriolic he got, over and over again. Mixed in with his relentless Jew-hating was some sort of jive about how their fellow Bundists, including him, were being unfairly prosecuted and harassed by the U.S. government, which made no sense, he said, because every last member was completely 100 percent American, wanting only the best for his wonderful country. Then he transferred his ire to President Roosevelt ("Rosenfeld"), claiming _he_ was Jewish (only he used a slur) and leading the people of the U.S.A. into slavery.

It all sounded like unremitting horse shit

to me, and although I tried to follow his reasoning, twisted as it was, I gave up after a while, tuned him out, and started staring at the back of Gena's head there in the front row, wondering what that cascading blonde hair would feel next to my cheek, and . . . well, you know.

Before I knew it, the diminutive speaker was done and bowing wildly to the crowd's standing ovation. I wondered how anyone could be deluded enough to buy into this whole nasty business, when it was pretty obvious to me that the bedrock of everything he said was a deep vein of fascist fool's gold.

The shindig broke up pretty quickly after that. A few people stuck around in front of the stage, talking to the speaker, including Elrich, Gena, and Fehring, and the other two women in attendance wandered over to the refreshment table and began cleaning up, both of them glancing back at me from time to time.

My seventh sense had calmed during the speech, but I still stayed in the background, just watching. I wasn't quite ready yet for Elrich to glad-hand me and ask me what I thought, because I wasn't sure what I was going to tell him. I didn't want to lie and tell him how lovely it was, but I figured I'd better not act offended either, as it looked to me like I'd be needing to explore this whole movement a little further — especially since my warning system had gone off like a rocket when Fehring showed up.

So, I actually stepped back a little, staying close to the wall, and, making myself as inconspicuous as possible, circled around to where Fehring, Gena, and Elrich stood with the puffed-up little speaker. Thanks to the barely adequate lighting, I didn't seem to be noticed. There was an open door there that led to some sort of storage room, and I squeezed myself in between the door and the wall and stood there, peering around. It looked like the perfect place to eavesdrop.

By this time, several of the Bund boys had already headed for the exits, off for who knows where. After a few more moments, the speaker excused himself from the group, making his way toward a door in the back of the room, Elrich yakking away by his side, matching him step for step.

That left Fehring and Gena alone. In a moment, I saw him gaze around the room. He seemed to be looking for someone, and the continued buzzing of my seventh sense indicated it was probably me. After a few moments of not spotting me, he motioned to the two guys who'd been guarding the speaker — the ones with the Browning belts and matching saps. When they joined him, he reached in his wallet, drew out some lettuce, and slipped each of them a double sawbuck, nodding toward the back. At first I thought this might have something to do with Elrich or the speaker instead of yours truly, but then I heard, distinctly, the words "this _Schweinhund_ Brown" and "can't be far." With their heads bobbing and big mean grins on their faces, those two clowns were about as subtle as the Ritz Brothers, and in a flash it became obvious to me what was going on. Immediately, they headed for the stairway that led up to the trap door in the floor of the jewelry store.

When they were gone, I saw Gena pluck at Fehring's sleeve, her mouth forming words. But although I tried as hard as I could, I had no idea what she was saying to him. The romantic in me wanted to think she was trying to talk him out of having me beaten up, or worse. I was sure that was why the cash had changed hands.

Whatever she was saying didn't seem to faze him, though. Taking her by the arm, he steered her toward the back of the room, where Elrich and the Nazi runt had gone a moment before. Now, the door was shut, and Elrich was standing outside it, his companion apparently having ditched him. In a moment, Fehring and Gena brushed by him, went in without knocking, and — pointedly, it seemed to me — shut the door in Elrich's face.

That was my cue to skedaddle. I sauntered out from behind the door, making sure that Elrich saw me.

"Hey, pally," he shouted. "_Mein freund._"

If he was disappointed about getting the

bum's rush, he didn't show it. As we clumped up the steps, he said, "Well, wha'd I tell ya? Somethin', ain't he?"

"He's something," I said.

"I just got done chewin' the fat with 'im," he said proudly. "We're buddies. The two of us, we think alike, ja."

I nodded, then gestured toward the stairway. "Those fellows in the brown shirts and Sam Browne belts — how come they're not dressed like the rest of you guys?"

He grinned, and the glint I saw in his eyes wasn't very pretty. "They're O.D.," he said, as if that explained everything.

"O.D.?"

"Ja. <u>Ordnungsdienst</u>. Bodyguards. Tough guys, ja." (O.K., I admit it. I looked up how to spell "ordnungsdienst" in a German-American dictionary after I got home.)

I nodded as we reached the floor of the jewelry store. Bending his considerable bulk, he made sure the trap door was back in place and slid a rug over it, while the same guy who'd opened the outside door for us when we entered stood aside silently, watching, and then led us back through the display cases.

Unlocking the door to the street, he opened it without so much as a word of farewell. As we stepped out into the night, I looked around, knowing what I was going to find. And, sure enough, there were the two

Ritz Brothers, still dressed in their Nazi finery, dour, hostile faces looming up out of the semi-darkness. The taller one had dark, curly hair; the other, who was thicker and shorter, was a short-cropped blond who looked mighty Aryan.

Just about then, a premonition skittered through me like a flash of lightning. But it was really unnecessary this time. I knew they had blood in their eyes. _My_ blood, of course.

It was obvious that Elrich didn't know their names, and he didn't introduce me. Instead, he began jabbering enthusiastically to them about the evening's speaker, how "he gave it to dem kikes and dat Jew Rosenfeld, huh." I wandered away from the trio and peered in the jewelry-store window. What I was really doing was watching their reflections as they stood behind me, and, sure enough, I saw Curly contort his face and give a quick nod toward where I stood. The angle was such that I couldn't quite get Elrich's response, but it looked to me like he simply shrugged.

The three of them came up behind me, Elrich said something about the sparklers in the store window, and then we headed out down the deserted sidewalk toward the trolley stop a few blocks away. As I think I told you earlier, it was a nicer section of town, with no bars or honky-tonks to draw people at this time of night, so I began wondering what would happen when — not if — I got jumped by the two who'd had their palms greased by the weird-eyed Nazi. Would there be a beat cop nearby? Might there be another pedestrian or two, or a cab driver, who might be willing to help me? This part of town seemed awfully uninhabited.

I didn't figure I could count on Elrich to take my side. There seemed to be more than a little hero worship in the way he approached those two.

While I was pondering all this, maybe half a block up the street, a door opened. In the stillness of the night, it creaked like the beginning of an _Inner Sanctum_ broadcast. Underneath the overhead light, a man shuffled out, carrying something.

"Hey, look," stage-whispered Curly. "That old sheeny Gold. That Jew boy tailor."

"Yeah," said the other. "What's that he's got?"

It was the first time I'd heard them speak, and I confess it was something of a shock to hear them speaking American English. I guess I'd figured them to be from the Fatherland.

That surprise came right on the heels of a second one. I suddenly realized that the man up the street under that light was the same Mr. Gold who'd smoked one of my Berings with me on the train, telling me gratefully that he'd fix me up with some new threads if I came and saw him at his store. And now, here he was again.

What were the chances?

Apparently, John, they were pretty damned good.

"That ol' hebe's carrying a bank bag!" said the first guy.

"No shit!" That was Elrich. And their exchange was so loud that they got Mr. Gold's attention, even from a half-block away. He turned, his glasses glinting yellow in the light from above his door, and peered through the darkness at us.

"Who's there?" he asked in a half-shout.

"You'll find out soon enough, kike!" answered Curly. I watched him slip that leather-covered lead sap — a "drum stick" — out of his Sam Browne belt and, thwacking it against his palm a couple of times, advance toward Mr. Gold. And then, _sotto voce_ to us, "It's Jew-beatin' time."

"I'll bet he's got his whole day's take in that bag — maybe more," said Elrich excitedly. "Here, _meine Freunde_, is where we can combine pleasure with business."

I know I don't have to describe the internal whirling dervish my seventh sense had become. The thing was, I wasn't exactly sure what route to take.So I held up my hand, locked eyes with Curly, and said, "Are you _nuts_? You use that sap, it's going to be armed robbery. You know what happens if they catch us?"

"They ain't _gonna_ catch us," Curly said, staring defiantly back at me and slapping the drum stick into his palm for emphasis.

Elrich looked from one of us to the other. Beside him, I saw the other O.D. pull his own blackjack out.

I shook my head. "Not me," I said, and made to leave the group. "I get caught doing something like this, I lose my job."

At the same time, I was thinking hard. If I got away, would I be able to find a cop in time? Or should I just stay and do my best against the odds? Mr. Gold was going to be attacked as sure as sunrise. I couldn't just leave him there, even to rouse a beat cop.

Stepping in front of me and raising his hand, Elrich helped me make up my mind. The grin I'd seen so many times suddenly looked like a snarl.

"Naw, pally," he said. "This'll be — well, call it an <u>initiation.</u> Help me and the boys here beat up that Jew bastard, and you're in, <u>ja</u>?"

His hand came down then, poking me in the chest with a forefinger. And suddenly, I saw my slovenly next-door neighbor for what he really was. Not just a deluded, half-bright goofball, more to be pitied than scorned, but an ugly, brutal Nazi sympathizer.

"You're with us, ain'tcha — <u>pally</u>?" he said, punching me again, his eyes indicating that I had little choice.So I forced a grin.

"Sure," I told him.

With that, he turned into the old hail-fellow-well-met Elrich again, slapping me on the back.

"Attaboy," he said. "Let's get that damned kike!"

As we advanced on Mr. Gold, my perspective switched and I thought how it must look through his eyes, four young men moving inexorably in on him like jackals about to attack a wounded animal. But I had to give the old boy credit. He didn't move a muscle. I wondered if he was too far from the doorway of his store to make a run for it and bolt himself in, and I found myself hoping he'd do just that.

We seemed frozen in time and darkness, but I knew we weren't. I could hear our footsteps echoing off the empty buildings, feel the chill wind past my face. Sticking my bare hands in the pockets of my CCC jacket, I felt a small hard cylinder with my left. It took me a moment to realize what it was: one of those rolls of four-bit coins I'd gotten in order to tip the porters back on the train. Gripping it gave me a feeling of security; a roll like that in a fist makes a pretty fair weapon.

Despite my hopes that Gold would seek the relative safety of his store, there was nothing doing on his end. He stood stock-still, just beside the curb, watching us as we closed the distance between him and us.

When we were maybe 20 feet away, Curly began thwacking the sap against his palm again, creating a staccato pattern that sounded oddly like a military drumbeat.

"Whatcha got in the bag, Jew boy?"

"It's none of your business," returned Mr. Gold defiantly. "Go home and leave me alone before I call the police."

Curly turned to us with a malevolent grin.

"Sure," he said. "We'll go home. But we're takin' your bag with us."

By this time, we were not far at all from Mr. Gold, and the three who were with me fanned out, surrounding him, the thunk-thunk-thunk of the drum stick slapping dully against Curly's palm. All their eyes were on him.

Mr. Gold's own eyes flickered from man to man, and then settled on me, registering surprise. I knew then that he remembered me.

Quickly, while the eyes of the others were on him, I risked a gesture, bringing my finger to my lips and nodding once. But I got caught.

"Hey," shouted the buzz-cut blond to me. "You <u>know</u> this kike?" I saw the blackjack, swinging easily in his hand.

"Yeah. I've seen him around," I returned, as casually as I could.

The guy's eyes narrowed as the other two turned to me. "That right?" he asked. "How come you're wanting him to be quiet? Hell, maybe <u>you're</u> a kike too."

And then, damned if Curly didn't laugh.

"Two birds," he said, slapping the sap once again as he advanced toward me. "Two birds with one stone." Then, to his companions, "You two get the old guy. I'll take care of this bastard."

Suddenly, the night air was shattered. "Help!" Mr. Gold yelled. "Police! Help!"

Well, that sure got Curly's attention. Advancing quickly on Mr. Gold, he swung that leather-covered blackjack up over his head, preparing to bring it down on the old man's skull. But before he could deliver the blow I leapt to his side, reached up, and grabbed the sap with my right hand, delivering a powerful left — aided by the roll of fifty-cent pieces — to a kidney. That loosened his grip on the drum stick. Wrenching it from his hand, I brought it down hard right behind his ear, and he staggered and dropped like he'd been poleaxed.

As I turned from him, a fist nailed me in the forehead, rocking me back and splashing a galaxy of swirling stars before my eyes. Dimly, I perceived the blond Nazi in front of me, cocking his arm and getting ready to bring the blackjack down across my neck. Before he could swing, he took a step back — the kind of mistake a lot of amateur street fighters make, keeping a distance between them and their opponents. From my time in the CCC, in the barracks and in the ring, I'd learned that you controlled the other guy by closing in, not backing off, and keeping an opponent close limited the force of his blows.So I lunged toward him, ducked a round-house swing with the blackjack hand, and shot a left into his soft belly. The roll of coins gave that punch a little extra authority, and as he sagged into me I threw a right to his throat, just under his chin.

"<u>Look out!</u>"

The shout came from Mr. Gold, and as my erstwhile opponent slid to the pavement, I whirled around to face Elrich, the easygoing mask gone, his face radiating pure hatred. As I squared off against him, I felt the guy I'd just dispatched grabbing at one of my ankles, so I looked down, saw where he was, and let loose a kick to his face.

Unfortunately, I watched him a split-second too long. The next thing I knew, a searing pain ripped through my body, brought on by a gut-punch from Elrich. I hadn't expected him to be able to hit quite that hard. The blow made me stumble, and my foot hit the now-still body on the pavement, causing me to lose my balance. I felt the sap fly out of my hand as I went down, but I had the presence of mind to roll away — just as a right hook from Elrich swished past my head. Grabbing his leg, I jerked him down. He was still swinging when he hit the pavement — and he bounced back up like a rubber ball.

By that time, I'd gotten to my feet as well, and we began trading blows. I saw quickly that what I'd thought was flabbiness in my next-door Nazi was really mostly muscle; his stomach was a lot harder than I thought it would be. Dancing back, I ducked a left jab and gave him my own left to his face. It landed with a satisfying <u>crunch</u>. His nose spurting blood, he shook his head like an injured bull and came at me, fists flailing. I threw a flurry back at him, but it didn't seem to do much good. About that time, I began feeling light headed. I knew he was getting the best of me, and, through a kind of haze, I started wondering if I was really licked this time and what that might mean to both me and Mr. Gold.

Then, I heard a metallic <u>thump</u>. And the rain of blows stopped.

Dead on my feet, I swayed, trying to bring things into focus. Then, I saw Mr. Gold, holding his bank bag, looking down. It must've had plenty of silver in it, along with the folding money, to make that kind of sound when it hit Elrich's head.

Like his two O.D. brothers, Elrich now reposed on the pavement, not moving. As I looked at him, I felt Mr. Gold's hand on my shoulder.

"We call the police, yes?" he said softly.

I considered that for a moment.

"No," I said. "That might bring more trouble than it's worth. They'd get out in a day or so, and they'd be so incensed about being locked up they might summon more forces and attack you again. Let's powder instead."

"It doesn't seem right."

"No sir. It's not right. But under the circumstances, I think it's best."

At that point, we began hearing a moan or two from our fallen adversaries, so I knew it was time to leave the scene. "C'm'on, Mr. Gold," I whispered. "Let's retreat to your store and watch."

He nodded. "Yes. It might not be prudent for me to make a night deposit at the bank right now."

"Prudent's the word," I said, as we crept away to his store and peered through the edge of the curtain at the door, seeing the three get up, shake their heads and look around, and then fade into the night. I thought they might be exercised enough to try and do something to Mr. Gold's store, maybe toss a paving brick or two through the window, but it didn't happen.

When they were gone, Mr. Gold turned to me.

"Robert, isn't it?" he asked.

"Yessir."

"Robert, I thank you again. I am in your debt twice."

I smiled at him. "Is that offer you gave me on the train still good? About the clothes, I mean?"

"The discount? Twice as good."

"Then I'll see you soon, right here in this store."

"It will be my pleasure," he said, unlocking the door and half-bowing.

I'd be lying if I didn't say that I kept to the shadows as I walked back toward my apartment building. I was lucky enough to catch a late trolley, and once I got to the building, I proceeded with an abundance of caution. For all I knew, they were waiting for me behind Elrich's door.

But when I got to my own room and put my ear to the wall, all was quiet. It's <u>still</u> quiet.

I guess maybe I'd tended to downplay the fight in my own mind, but now that I've written you about it, I can see that it's bigger and more important — and potentially more dangerous — than I thought. So now, instead of going to bed, I've made up my mind to pack up and find a hotel for a few days. Living in this nest of would-be Nazis has gotten dangerous enough for me to ankle this place.

The next time you hear from me, I'll have a different address. Unless, of course, Elrich and the boys jump me before I can get away. I don't want to be melodramatic, but if that happens, it's possible you could never hear from me again.

And on that happy note, I'll close.

Your faithful (and jittery) correspondent,

Robert

October 8, 1939
Sunday afternoon

Dear John,

I'll tell you frankly that the last time you heard from me, I was as nervous as ZaSu Pitts. That Friday morning, after I'd finished your letter, I got ready to go to work not knowing if I was going to be waylaid by a bunch of Bundists as soon as I opened the door. In fact, when I did crack it, I had that old cavalry Colt pistol at the ready — just in case.

But it was quiet as a tomb.So although I wasn't at my tip-top as far as pep goes, thanks to a mostly sleepless night, I went on to the War Department and a day's worth of work. Good old Mr. Fletcher with his buzzard breath greeted me, and I took the opportunity to ask him about hotels. To be honest, I blew him up a little bit in the process.

"Mr. Fletcher," I said, "you're a man who really knows his way around this town, and I'm wondering if you might be able to tell me the name of a hotel where I could stay for a few days — just until my boarding-house room is ready. I don't want to spend a fortune, but I'd like for it to be a reasonably clean and safe place, and one that's pretty close to here, where I might be able to walk to work and not have to take the trolley."

"Well, now, Mr. Brown," he returned, rubbing his chin. "Hotel rooms aren't easy to come by these days, what with all the military personnel we have coming into town. However, you might try the Davis. It's just a few blocks away, and I think it would cost you about two dollars a night — _if_ there are any rooms available."

I said that was fine. And, yes, I technically lied about the boarding house, but only technically. I've actually found one since then, which I'll tell you about after I lay out my Friday adventures.

So, during the noon hour, while enjoying my ice-cold Coke luncheon, I called up the Davis Hotel and got reservations for that night, plus a few days afterward. Of course, I let Fletch the Wretch know that I'd taken him up on his advice, and he seemed proud of that.

So, I had a hotel room. Cost: $1.75 per night. Paid for, mostly, by my secret Mackaville benefactor, Miss Mary Lou Castle, God bless her.

The next thing I had to do was get my things out of Crappy Towers — and, if at all possible, not to let the Bund boys know I was taking a run-out powder. I was pretty sure Elrich had some sort of job during the day, since he was only around his room at night. And I knew that some people here in D.C. were

working Saturday mornings as well as from
Monday through Friday. However, I couldn't
take a chance that my next-door neighbor was
one of them. To give myself the best chance
of slipping away undetected by him and his
goose-stepping buddies, I had no choice but
to ankle the place that afternoon.

My bags were pretty much packed and ready,
and I could get them all in one load. Would
Mr. Fletcher give me any time off that Friday
afternoon to move? Did I want to ask him, and
risk being turned down — or, maybe, given a
grilling about why I couldn't do it over the
weekend?

I pondered that, and to me there was only
one way I could stack the deck in my favor.
Finishing my Coke in a couple of gulps, I put
on the most pained face I could come up with,
got up, and walked past the desks that were
mostly empty during lunch. Fletcher had his
own office, and I figured he'd be in it.

Sure enough, when I knocked, I heard his
voice. Opening the door, I took in his lair.
Pretty spartan, with a big photo of President
Roosevelt on the wall and a desk with a few
framed pictures on it that I took to be wife
and kids. Spread in front of them was a big
cloth napkin with a partly eaten sandwich
atop it. And behind that was Mr. Fletcher,
the eyes under his Moe Howard bangs looking
quizzically up at me.

"Yes, Mr. Brown?"

"I'm sorry, Mr. Fletcher, but — well, I've

suddenly got a great deal of gastric distress." I put my hands across my stomach. "I don't feel well at all."

He shook his head, <u>tch-thching</u> me a couple of times. "I shouldn't wonder," he said. "I've noticed that you don't eat lunch. Soft drinks are no substitute for real, honest food, young man."

I nodded, screwing up my face even more. "I know," I said weakly. "May I be excused for a couple of hours? Maybe if I can just get home and lie down . . .

"Do you have anything to take?" he asked, and before I could answer he'd pulled open his top desk drawer and extracted a packet of Bromo-Seltzer, holding it out to me. "This should help," he said.

"I'm afraid I'm a little past that."

"Oh. I see," he said. And reaching in again, he brought out a small bottle of paregoric. "This, then?"

"Well . . ."

"You don't have to worry about my being squeamish, Mr. Brown. I was in the Army. Here. I'll get you a cup."

Of course, I knew what paregoric was for, John, and I quickly realized I was in a jam. You know how medicines sometimes work with me — they do the exact opposite of what they're supposed to. I didn't want to take a chance on the paregoric backfiring, if you know what I mean.

Maybe, I thought, I could ask if I could

just take the bottle home and bring it back tomorrow.

By then, however, he was already moving to the water cooler in the corner of his office, plucking a conical paper cup from the holder and returning to me.

"Now," he said, pouring a little of the viscous liquid into the cup. "Just take this. And perhaps you'd be better off going home immediately. This stuff goes to work in a jiffy."

I grabbed it from him, swallowed down its contents, and muttered out a "thank you" before turning and heading out of his office, almost in a run. I knew a little something about paregoric, too, and if it was really going to work in reverse on me, I was aware that every second counted.

I'll draw a veil over the next several hours, except to say that even though I got the reverse effect I feared from the medication, I managed to get everything out of there, into a cab, and, with the help of a bellhop, into my new hotel room at the Davis Hotel, which appears to be a pretty decent middle-class joint. I had to take, shall we say, frequent breaks, but I managed to get everything stacked off to the side of the Crappy Towers door and find a cabbie to help me load up. Then I turned in my key at the front desk and skedaddled.

Of course, I couldn't be sure that I hadn't been spotted by any of the Bundists, but if any were around, they weren't making themselves apparent to <u>me</u>. And I didn't think they'd follow me once I got into my cab. Still, I watched out the back window all during the trip, looking for anything suspicious. Off and on along the way to the hotel, little thrills went through me that I thought could be the seventh sense, but then I chalked it up to my feeling like I was in a Warner Brothers gangster movie. The fact that the hackie was an almost dead ringer for Allen Jenkins didn't help matters any.

I got myself and my baggage to my room on the eighth floor without further incident, tipped the wizened old bellhop two bits, and laid down on the nice big bed in what was a pretty comfy room. The radiator was purring nicely over against the wall, sending out warmth against the gathering chill of the evening, and, best of all, the paregoric seemed to have finally gotten through my system. I started to float away into an untroubled sleep.

And that's where I was, floating gently above all my troubles, when the phone rang.

(I break here for dramatic effect.)

You remember that old tale we heard when we were kids, supposedly the shortest story ever written? "A woman is alone in the world. She knows she is the only person on earth who's still alive. The 'phone rings."

I felt like that woman. The ringing pulled me up out of my sleep, and I stared at the instrument beside the bed with horror. Honestly, at that time I couldn't have told you whether it was the seventh sense or just sheer panic that surged through me. No one knew I was here, and I knew no one knew.

Later, I realized that it could've been the desk clerk or someone similarly innocuous. That possibility didn't occur to me at the time, though, and all I could think to do as I picked up the receiver was disguise my voice. Poorly, as it turned out.

"Yess. Who iss calling, please?" I said in what I thought would pass as a Germanic accent.

There was a long pause — long enough for me to look at the clock on the end table and see that I'd only been asleep a couple of hours. Then, I heard a giggle on the other end of the line.

Then, the smoky voice of Gena Laubauch, unmistakable. "You are really funny, Robert Brown," she said. "I hope you weren't actually trying to fool anyone."

I was still attempting to clear the fog from my head when she added, "Look. I need to talk with you now, but I'm still at work. Do you know Woodies — Woodward and Lothrop? That's where I'll be. Fourth floor. Notions department. I'll watch for you to get off the elevator."

Finally, I found my voice.

"Gena," I said. "How in the hell did you find me?"

"You were followed," she said. "One of the Bundists just happened by a few minutes ago. He couldn't help bragging about how they tailed you to the Davis and, as he put it, were now going to 'deal' with you in the name of the Fatherland."

"Thanks for the warning, Gena. Why do you need to see me?"

"I'll tell you when you get here. Please hurry. And remember: You're being watched."

"I'm on my way," I told her.

Taking a little time to throw some water on my face, I checked myself in the mirror above the basin and unpacked a brush to run through my hair. When I opened the suitcase, I saw that envelope full of cash from Miss Castle, and stuffed some lettuce in my pocket.

Something — maybe my seventh sense, maybe not — told me to put on my CCC uniform instead of regular clothes, so I did. Then I went out the door fast, half-expecting someone to be waiting outside with a sap — or worse. My old cavalry pistol was still in a suitcase, but the way I felt, I could get by with the help of my seventh sense — and my fists, if it came to that.

No one was in the hallway. I got on the

elevator, which was almost full, and worked my way back against the wall. The door opened on the seventh floor to pick up someone else, and in the small space between a couple of my fellow passengers, I saw three guys smoking beside the stairwell. They peered into the elevator. They weren't in uniform, but I've always been pretty good with faces, and I recognized them from the Bund meeting. Even if I hadn't, the jittering of my seventh sense would've tipped me off.

I made myself as invisible as I could, squeezing behind a big woman with a huge purse, and after a mother and her little boy got off, the operator closed the doors.

The seventh-sense waves had risen a little, pulsing inside me, and I felt pretty sure they were warning me to avoid the lobby.So I exited at the third floor and carefully made my way down the stairs to the basement. Once I'd left the main floor behind, the feeling faded, letting me know I'd guessed right.

The head janitor had a little basement office, and he happened to be sitting inside it in his undershirt, reading a western pulp, when I came up and knocked lightly at his door. I made sure he spied the twin dollar bills sticking up out of my closed hand.

"Help you?" he asked, eyeing them.

"Yes sir," I returned. "My name's Robert Brown. I just moved in. And I'd be very interested if you could show me how I'd get out of this building through the basement."

His eyes narrowed, but they stayed on the bills. "You some sort of spy?" he asked.

"Not exactly." I grinned. "Let's call it dame problems."

He had his considerable bulk up and out of his chair and the two checkers snatched from my grasp almost before I knew it, his grin showing a couple of missing teeth. "C'm'on," he said. "Always glad to help a fellow sheik." Then he winked, pointing to a door, and pressed a key into my hand.

"It's an extra," he told me. "Fetch it back when you can. Exit at the other end. Key works 'em both. Watch your step."

I nodded and went through the door into a dark storage area. By lighting a few matches, I was able to pick my way through the trunks, boxes, and other dusty old junk to a door under a red "exit" light. I paused a moment, taking stock of my seventh sense, which now seemed to be bubbling a little but not boiling, if you know what I mean.

As I opened the door and stepped out into the little alcove with steps leading up to the sidewalk, I thought, well, a disguise would've been helpful. But it was too late now. If any of the junior Nazis were outside watching the doors, I had to count on the hope that they wouldn't be watching this one.

Sure enough, I spotted one at the corner of the hotel, maybe 100 yards away from me.

Even in street clothes, he was recognizable as one of the guys I'd been around at the meeting, Thin as Ichabod Crane and just about as appealing, he'd been one of the bozos trying so hard to impress Gena and the other two Bund frails.

Now, he was doing his best to look inconspicuous, leaning up against the brick facing at the corner of the hotel and keeping his head craned around, watching the front entrance. He was as gawky as a stork, and if the situation hadn't been so serious, I might have burst out laughing. Instead, I did a little reconnoitering from my alcove, confident that I hadn't been seen. Although I didn't spot any of his Bund pals anywhere around, I knew they could be out there, just waiting for me to show myself.

I was considering my options when, suddenly, I got a break. A taxi pulled up just in front of the cafe next door, less than a stone's throw away from my hiding place beneath the sidewalk, and debouched two gaily chatting couples. I waited for the final guy out to pay the cabbie, and when he turned to walk away and join his party, I took the few steps at a jump and ran for the car, throwing open the back door.

"Get me out of here fast!" I shouted, pitching a buck at him over the top of the seat. Behind me, I heard a yell and looked up to see my tail breaking for the taxi.

Then, a second bit of good luck hit. The

hackie turned his head toward me, and it was the same guy who'd chauffeured me from Crappy Towers to the hotel — the Allen Jenkins lookalike. When he saw it was me, he grinned, stuffing the greenback in his front pocket.

"Nice to see you again, chief," he said. "Where you going?"

"Anywhere out of <u>here</u>," I said, looking out the back window at Ichabod Hitler, who was running toward us, a small automatic pistol in his hand. "And sooner rather than later."

He followed my line of sight.

"Hey, that guy's got a roscoe," he said. "He ain't a cop, is he?"

"Hell, no," I blurted out. "He's a Nazi — a Bund. I had a row with 'em, and they want my scalp."

I don't know if Ichabod ever fired, since the sudden squeal of tires drowned out all other sounds, including something that sounded like "hang on, chief," from my driver. But if the skinny Bundist had happened to squeeze a shot or two off, he'd missed us. When I located him again, he was standing on the sidewalk, watching as we put distance between us and him, his angry face receding quickly to the size of a dot.

"Looks like you shook him," I said, settling back. "Thanks."

"Never have liked gettin' shot at," he returned. "Especially by a Nazi. Got no use for 'em."

"You and me both." The hum of the cab's motor slowed a bit, as he geared down to a more normal speed, falling in with the late-afternoon traffic.

"Going anywhere in particular, or just away from <u>that</u> gink?"

I remembered, then, what Gena had told me.

"A place called Woodies," I said. "Know it?"

"Who don't?"

I'd barely gotten the time to look at his license, hanging from the rear-view mirror, before we pulled up in front of a big ten-story edifice whose sign identified it as the Woodward & Lothrop building. I caught his gaze in the front-seat mirror.

"Thanks," I said. "What do I owe you?"

"You paid for the trip, chief, and then some. We're even."

"The dollar was a tip. You got me out of a jam, and I appreciate it."

"Well, thanks. Sixty cents ought to do it."

Fishing another single out of my wallet, I passed it to him over the top of the seat. "Keep the change," I said.

That one disappeared in his front pocket as well, and he nodded his thanks. I nodded back, opened the back door, and started for the building. But as I started past the cab, he rolled down the passenger-side window and stopped me.

"Hey, chief," he said. "Like I said, I

ain't no Nazi lover neither — especially them phony Nazis. If you ain't gonna be gone too long, I can stick around, kind of keep an eye out. I don't think we was followed, but there's always that chance."

I grinned in spite of myself. "What'll it cost me?" I asked.

"You been fair to me. Whatever you think it's worth."

"Deal," I said, and stuck out my hand. He shook it. "You stick around, and I'll be back. Where can I find you?"

He nodded toward a taxi stand fifty or so feet down the block.

"Okay. See you in a little while." I started away, then stopped and stuck out my hand again, remembering the name I'd seen on his license. "By the way, Mike. My name's Robert. Robert Brown."

"I'm Smokey Stover," he said, gripping my hand again. "My license says 'Mike,' but everyone calls me 'Smokey' — just like in the funny pages."

"Nice to meet you, Smokey — and thanks again."

"Ain't nothin', chief," he said. "I'll be around."

The inside of Woodward & Lothrop's was filled with early-evening shoppers, which I figured was a good deal, since I wouldn't be spotted as easily if anyone really was looking for me. I found the elevator and went up to the fourth floor, as Gena had instructed me to do in her telephone call.

I honestly believe, John, that I could've closed my eyes and followed the trail of Shalimar right to her station, where she stood showing a woman a selection of scarves. Taking up a position at the end of the glass counter, I saw her look up with a glimmer of recognition as she gently put the merchandise into a gift box. I nodded back and watched as she rang up the sale, thanked the customer, and then ambled over to where I stood. Even at the end of the day, the Shalimar was still potent.

"I've been off the clock for almost ten minutes," she said, by way of greeting. "And I'm hungry. Let's get out of here."

When she stepped out from behind the counter, I bowed slightly and took her arm.

"I've got a cab waiting. May I buy your supper tonight?"

She smiled and squeezed my hand. "Of course, but I have to warn you. I'm not a cheap date."

"Neither am I."

She laughed at that and went to a door in the back of the floor. When she came out, she had on a white, fur-collared coat. It went well with her complexion and that cascading blonde hair.

I have to admit that with this intoxicating young woman on my arm I didn't think much about the Bund or being tailed as the elevator let us off at the ground floor. But since I didn't detect any seventh-sense stirrings, I figured I was safe enough.

Smokey and his cab were right where he said he'd be, and as we got in, I saw him surreptitiously sizing up Gena and liking what he saw.

"Gena," I said as we settled in, "I'm a stranger here in the City of Magnificent Intentions. Would you please tell Mr. Stover here where we're going?"

"Certainly. And I'm glad to see you're acquainted with Dickens. He's one of my favorite authors."

She watched me long enough to see my look of surprise, and then languidly leaned forward and told Smokey that we'd be going to the Mayfair.

Apparently, I was the only one in the cab who didn't know the place. But when I asked her about it, she dismissed my question with a, "You'll know soon enough, and I think you'll like it," adding, "But let's talk about why I called you."

I settled back into the seat. "All right," I said. "Let's."

It was getting to be dusk, and her blue eyes picked up the passing lights of the city as Smokey wove expertly in and out of traffic.

"Robert," she said. "When you smacked those three guys down you bought yourself some trouble. It's serious. They're planning on killing you, and soon."

Although she spoke in little more than a whisper, I felt sure that Smokey was listening in. Maybe that was for the best. I needed all the allies I could muster.

Forcing a smile, I asked, "Why are you telling me this, Gena?"

She looked away then, the city's shadows still flitting by her face. "You impress me," she said. "And . . . there are other reasons."

"For instance?"

She still wasn't looking at me. "Some I'm not ready to tell you. Maybe I should just say I've grown, I don't know, <u>disenchanted</u> with the movement, and the people in it. I'm seeing them for what they are, and they're like rattlesnakes." She turned then, fixing me with her eyes. "I know you think you can take care of yourself, but please — watch out. Beating them up like you did struck deep at their pride, and they won't be happy until they have your neck."

"You know," I said, as casually as I could make it, "two of 'em were hired by your boyfriend."

She blanched at that, a blush spreading across her cheeks as she once again looked away. Her "yes . . . my boyfriend" was muffled almost to silence.

I suddenly felt bad for bringing that up. And not only that. When she'd muttered those words, I'd felt a little current of the seventh sense skitter through me — enough for me to know something was wrong.

Touching her shoulder, I said softly, "Look. Trust me. If they try anything else they'll be devoutly wishing they'd never messed with me. I give you my word on that — but that better be all I tell you."

She exhaled, once again facing me. "I think you mean that," she said. "So, I'll stop worrying."

I started to ask her if she was worried about anything else, but then I realized that Smokey had slowed his chariot to a full stop.

"We're here," she said, nodding toward the imposing building on our right.

I helped her out of the car and then went around to pay Smokey, who stage-whispered as he took my bill, "You really cool _three_ of them pocket Nazis? All at once?" When I nodded yes, he whistled so loudly that Gena, on the sidewalk, turned to look.

"You're jake by me, chief," he said. "Want me to come by and pick you up in, oh, let's say an hour and a half?"

"Sure thing — and here." I handed him two fives out of the stash I'd pocketed back at the hotel, but he handed me one back.

"Don't spoil me," he said with a grin. "See you in ninety minutes, give or take."

The Mayfair was really something, John. A supper club, Gena told me, with lots of different kinds of entertainment later on. We got there a little bit before six, which I saw was early for the dinner crowd; it was still the cocktail hour. On Gena's recommendation, we ordered up a couple of zombies, which were big drinks, fruity and full of alcohol. I'd heard of 'em but never had one; Gena said she'd been introduced to them at the World's Fair when she'd visited New York back in the summer.

We were served by a beautiful waitress dressed all in Dutch garb, right down to the wooden shoes. She was just one of the girls who were busy serving drinks and food — drinks, mostly — and all of them were dressed in outfits that represented different nations. The whole place was definitely cosmopolitan and, really, kind of exotic, from the chrome tables and fixtures to the big murals on the walls that showed scenes from around the world and featured a painted row of flags from all countries. I wondered how long it might be before someone would have to paint over the German one.

I was surprised to see that their dinner menu was limited. I think if we'd gotten there later, during the official dinner hour, we would've had more selections, but as it was we only had three or four. As it turned out, that was all we needed. Gena got the filet mignon with sauteed mushrooms — rare, and she really tore into it — and I took a chance on something called Roast Beef New York, which came with lots of brown gravy as well as a bowl of <u>au jus</u>. I've never really associated gravy with the Big Apple, but it was plenty good.

We dined like a king and queen, and while we did, we talked about things that I guess any couple would talk about on their first time out to dinner together. Turned out that she was from Milwaukee, which went a long way toward explaining her Germanic heritage. Like me, she'd graduated from college and then, because of the Depression, had to go to work. I found out a lot about her without ever getting too personal, and while the zombies had been plenty potent, neither one of us got uninhibited enough to ask any embarrassing questions.

Not that I didn't think about it. I wondered exactly what she was doing here with me when she was allegedly Fehring's doll, and why she was warning me about the Bundists when she was one of 'em. But I let myself give in to the warm feeling brought on by the alcohol, a good meal, the scent of Shalimar, and her downright alluring presence across the table.

Then, the mood abruptly changed.

"Robert," she said, averting her eyes and swallowing hard, "may I tell you something that could very well be impossible for you to understand? It's something I don't even understand myself."

"Of course, Gena."

"You mentioned my . . . <u>boyfriend</u> a while

ago. You probably can see that he's older than me. <u>Much</u> older." Still not looking at me, she began tapping her finger on the table, nervously. "And I want to be free from him."

Then she looked up. "But he has a <u>hold</u> on me."

"I understand. It happens."

She shook her head, looking back down at the table. "No. You <u>don't</u> understand. This is not a hold that some aging roue would have on a smitten schoolgirl. This is something else. Something far more sinister."

Inside me, alarm bells began to ring.

When she looked up again, her eyes were shiny with suppressed tears. But her voice was strong and unwavering. "He is something more than human. Something <u>other</u>. I want to get away. But I <u>can't</u>."

Even as I took her hands across the table, I <u>knew</u>, John. I suppose I'd known ever since he and I had locked eyes in the basement of the jewelry store. The seventh-sense flashing inside me as I touched her confirmed it. Like Gena said, her boyfriend Fehring was something more than human, all right. He was a lycanthrope — part-animal and part-human — and the sense of wolfishness I'd felt from him that evening confirmed it. I now knew what he was as well as I knew my own name.

"Gena," I said, still holding onto her hands, "all you have to know is this. I can help. If you want me to, I can help."

"But you don't know—"

"I know enough. Remember when I told you that it would be bad for any of those Bund yokels to attack me?"

She nodded, swallowing.

"I may be a little more than human, too," I said. "That's all you really need to know."

Silently, she looked into my eyes. It seemed like hours before she said, "I believe you."

"Good."

"So now, we'll talk about something else."

"Sure." I let go of her hands and she took a deep breath.

"What's your favorite motion picture?" she asked and laughed. "Mine's <u>The Wizard of Oz</u>. I've seen it four times since it came out, and I'm probably going to go another couple of times. Maybe you'd take me?"

Just like that, the tension broke, both outside and inside of me, my seventh sense calming. And although we didn't speak about Fehring any more that evening, I knew that at some point I was going to have to confront him, and that it would take a good deal of magic for me to come out on top.

Although she'd made noise about being an expensive date, the meals — with appetizers and desert included — only came to a couple of bucks. They nailed us a little on the zombies — $1.25 each — but those were worth it, too. I gave our little Dutch girl seven bucks for everything, including the tip, and she seemed delighted. When we arose, Gena gently put her hand on my arm, and I as escorted her out, through the murals and the gaily clad waitresses and the gathering crowd, I felt like a million bucks.

Smokey Stover was waiting for us, motor running. After I'd helped Gena into the back seat, she leaned forward, gave her address, and in too few minutes, we were slowing down in front of an apartment house.

It was a decent place, in a good part of town, and I started to get out to escort her to the door. She stopped me with a squeeze of my hand.

"No, Robert," she said. "They may be watching, and you could get us both in very bad trouble."

I had to admit she was right. "Okay," I told her.

Leaning in suddenly, she kissed me on the cheek. "Thank you for a very nice evening," she said, and passed me a slip of paper. On it, she'd written her telephone number.

"In case you want to take me to see <u>The Wizard of Oz</u>," she said with a smile, and then she was out and gone and Smokey was pulling away from the curb. I watched out the back window as she walked up the stairs and opened the door. There were wisps of fog in my brain that had little to do with the zombie, and through them I half-expected to see someone detach himself from the shadows and follow her in. The funny thing was, I wasn't sure whether they'd be out to get her or they'd be on her side, maybe part of some elaborate scheme to trap me.

Still, if she'd wanted to give me away to the junior-league Nazis, why had she warned me about them? And why had she not let me walk her to her door? Could Fehring have something to do with all of this? Was her confession about his power over her real, or some sort of trick to draw me into her web, where he could attack me with her complicity?

What my seventh sense had told me at the restaurant was that something well outside the ordinary was going on with her, that Fehring was indeed a supernatural creature — a lycanthrope. What it _didn't_ tell me was whether or not she was sincere about wanting to get out. My seventh sense indicated that she was, but it had all happened so fast that I needed time to sort it out.

Smokey turned right and Gena's apartment building disappeared in front of my eyes, replaced by the busy tableau of Washington D.C. after dark: cars honking, pedestrians hurrying, lights shining in rows of buildings. Lost in my thoughts about Gena and her motives, I became aware that Smokey was speaking to me.

"Sorry, Smokey," I said, turning my gaze away from the rear window and settling into the seat. "What was it you were saying?"

He chuckled. "I don't blame you for being

discombooberated, chief. She's some dish. And that perfume — oh, boy."

"Yeah, I guess I'm a lucky guy," I said.

"<u>Lucky</u>," he snorted. "Hell. If you don't mind me saying so, you're <u>well</u> past lucky."

"I don't mind."

"When do we pick her up again?" he asked. "It'll give me something to look forward to."

It seemed to take minutes before I answered, and it was simply because I wasn't sure what to say.

<u>When do we pick her up again?</u>

"I wish I knew, Smokey," I said finally. "Maybe never."

Behind the wheel, he shook his head like a punch-drunk prizefighter. "Aw, chief," he said, and there was something like pity in his voice. "I sure as hell hope you're wrong."

Then, he reached over the seat and handed me a business card, saying, "Here's the number for my dispatcher. When you want me again, give me a call — especially if you've got that wonderful lookin' quail with you."

He winked and I nodded and got out, returning his smile. And that looks like a good place to close for now — even though, amazingly enough, there's still lots more to tell you about what turned out to be a hell of a weekend.

In fact, right now I'm fooling with the idea of calling in sick to Mr. Fletcher tomorrow morning, just so I can recover from it all. If I did, and I wrote you for another hour or two, I might be able to catch you up. I'm not kidding. This letter could be another <u>Gone with the Wind</u>.

Right now, though, I'll take a breather. I'll be back with you soon for Chapter Two: <u>Human Targets</u> (with my usual apologies to just about every Republic Studios serial ever made).

Your faithful correspondent,
Robert

October 8, 1939 (continued)
Sunday evening

Dear John,

I barely got that last missive into an envelope without busting it at the seams, so I'll mail this one separately. And I'll try to be a little less logorrheic. It was Shakespeare, wasn't it, who said brevity was the soul of wit? I'm afraid I haven't been very witty with you.

So here are the high spots: When I got up Saturday morning, donned my CCC uniform again — right or wrong, it gives me a kick to see people respond to me like I'm a serviceman — and checked a copy of the <u>Washington Times Herald</u> down in the hotel's lobby, I figured I must be living right. The classifieds had a listing for a boarding-house room at 60 clams a month, and once I lamped that I didn't let any grass grow under my feet. Using the Ameche in the lobby, I called the dispatcher, and Smokey Stover was out front in his hack almost before I hung up. Of course, he expressed his disappointment about Gena not being along for the ride. But he didn't let that little fact get in the way of his speeding me toward my destination like Barney Oldfield, all the while keeping up a running commentary about how it was a decent neighborhood, with hard-working good salt-of-the-earth people, and letting me know how lucky I'd be if I actually got it.

"There's a housing shortage in this burg, chief," he said, "and don't think for a minute you're the only gazabo looking hard for a place to hang his hat."

He had me so worked up by the time we pulled up in front of the place that I flew from his back seat like I'd been shot out of a cannon. I actually ran to the porch of the place, a nice old two-story house, well kept-up, that reminded me a little bit of Ma Stean's back in Arkansas.

The woman who came to the door didn't look a thing like Ma, though. She looked more like a cotton-wrapped yardstick with a head on top, sporting a sharp-featured face with a corvine nose. When she answered the door, I breathlessly told her I was responding to her newspaper ad, and did she still have that room available?

She looked me up and down with a sour countenance that reminded me of Margaret Hamilton in _The Wizard of Oz_. And then, surprisingly, she smiled a nice smile.

"I admire your enthusiasm, young man," she told me. "I watched you run up here. You must really want that room."

"Yes, ma'am," I countered.

"Well, since you're the first one here, it's yours."

My sigh of relief was a little louder than

I would've liked, but it was genuine. Then, she lifted a finger.

"That is, if you're not a felon or a spy." Looking around furtively, she whispered, "I hear there are lots of spies in town these days — Germans and such." Then, she seemed to pause, as though a thought had just entered her head. Narrowing her eyes, she asked, "Now, you're not German, are you, Mister — ?"

"Brown. Robert A. Brown. And yes ma'am, I won't lie to you, I've got a lot of German ancestors, but I'm 100 percent American. I grew up in Minnesota and I was in the CCC. This is my old CCC uniform."

She nodded as though she were seeing it for the first time. Smiling again, she said, "Well, that's good enough for me. When do you want to move in?"

I looked back toward Smokey's taxi, rumbling at the curb, with its driver peering out at us. I gave him the "OK" sign.

"Immediately," I said, "if that's all right with you." When she nodded, I added, "I'll be back with my bags and all just as soon as I can check out of my hotel. And thank you. I'm grateful."

Smokey and I were halfway across town before I realized I hadn't even asked her name.

Turns out it was Mrs. Dean. When I got back with all my stuff, she directed me to a room on the second floor — which, she said, is where all the boarders lived. (This being

Saturday, none of 'em were there at the time.) The space she showed me to was in the northeast corner of the boarding house, and it was pretty typical: desk, bed, chest of drawers, closet, and two windows, one looking west and one north. Again, it was a lot like Ma Stean's — I guess all boarding houses look pretty much the same — but not quite as spacious, the ceilings a little lower. The furniture was a long way from being new, but it was in pretty good shape. There was one shared bathroom, which I'd figured on, and she showed me that as well, along with the dining area downstairs.

There was one atypical thing about it, though. She explained that when new safety laws had been passed in the District of Columbia several years ago, she'd had to put in a fire escape in back of the house and make sure that everyone who lived there had access to it. That meant I had to keep my door unlocked at all times, because the only way anyone could get to that emergency exit was through my room. She opened my back door to show me a little porch with a railing, the stairs underneath it zig-zagging down the side of the building.

Of course, she'd neglected to tell me about all of that when I'd first said I wanted the room, and maybe it might have scotched the deal for some people, especially those who covet their privacy and don't relish someone being able to walk in on 'em at any time. But it didn't bother me. I figured my seventh sense would make a good enough alarm if danger threatened — and, honestly, my days in the barracks at CCC camps had long ago knocked any necessity for privacy out of me.

When I told Mrs. Dean I'd have no trouble keeping the door unlatched, she seemed visibly relieved. I wondered if maybe she'd shown it to others who didn't like the setup. But it didn't matter. Locks or no locks, this was my home for me now.

While we were going back up the stairs to my room, she asked me what I did for a living, and I told her about my job and also that I was a writer, because I didn't want her to hear me typing away at odd hours and start wondering. She said that was fine, but if I was going to do much writing in my room that I ought to get one of those rubber pads to put my typer on, so the noise wouldn't disturb the other boarders. I promised her I would.

Once she left, it didn't take me long at all to unpack and get everything put in its proper place. She'd told me that I was on my own for lunch on Saturdays, even though she'd have breakfast and a cold supper available, but if I needed a sandwich or something today she could probably fix me up. I told her no, I was going into town, and after she directed me to a spot where I could catch the street-car, off I went. Putting what clothes I had in the drawers and on hangers reminded me that I hardly had a week's worth of changes — and, since I didn't wear my old CCC duds to work, I figured now would be a good time to see just how much Mr. Hyrum Gold appreciated not only the stogie I'd given him on the train, but also the fight I'd put up against the Bund members who'd been threatening him a few nights ago.So I put on a fresh CCC uniform, grabbed up my jacket, and headed out.

Hy's Clothes for Men had that good old haberdashery smell that we both remember from Maupin's Clothing back in Hallock, and the bell above its door had barely stopped tinkling when I heard Mr. Gold's voice, so loud and warm that it almost embarrassed me.

"Mr. Brown! Mr. Brown! How good of you to come!"

And then, there he was in the wooden aisle, moving quickly between hanging suits and bins of shirts and underwear, shooing away a saleslady who'd started toward me. Grabbing my hand in both of his, he said, "I'm so pleased that you honor my humble store."

I looked around. The interior was considerably bigger, and far more upscale, than our hometown Maupin's.

"Humble, my eye," I said, grinning. "You've really got something here; I just hope I can afford to shop with you."

He grinned back. "Please. You will always

get the same ten percent discount I give to my employees — and, of course, if you need anything on credit, I am at your disposal."

"I guess you have a pretty good idea of my financial state, huh?"

He let that go by and instead asked what he could do for me.

"I believe I need a tailored jacket," I told him. "Maybe two. Plus, some shirts and slacks."

Nodding, he took me across the floor to a rack of good-looking dress jackets. I turned the price tag over on one, saw that it said $49.95, and told him, "A little rich for my blood, I'm afraid. I might be able to afford about half that."

Again, the smile. "Interestingly enough, Mr. Brown, you can have any of these you desire for the sale price of $24.50."

Wowsa, what a deal. I bought three — thank you again, Miss Mary Lou Castle — and then went over and picked up six dress shirts and three slacks — which, he said, also happened to be on sale for half-price, as were the socks and extra underwear I got. I'd budgeted 150 simoleons for my new wardrobe, and, with the 10 percent "employee" discount he insisted on factoring in, I got out of there for under 100. That cost included Mr. Gold himself taking a few measurements and telling me he'd tailor the jackets so that they'd fit perfectly.

I was so taken with my purchases and Mr.

Gold's largesse that it took me a while to realize something was going on outside the store — and inside <u>me</u>, as my internal alarm system had started a small but insistent buzzing. The customers and sales people tried to act as though there were nothing untoward happening, but their eyes kept flashing toward the store window, which opened onto the sidewalk where the ruckus seemed to be located.

Curious, I went to the window and immediately lamped what was going on. I guess the Bund members hadn't gotten the message after our earlier nighttime encounter outside this same store, because here they were again, about a dozen of the little bastards, all guys, identically dressed in their black-and-white getups with the red symbols on their caps. They carried signs, mostly hand lettered. And while I didn't see the two O.D guys I'd tangled with on that night, damned if I didn't spot my erstwhile next-door neighbor, Elrich, holding up a big piece of cardboard that sported the lovely sentiment "Protect America! Jews are aliens!" With some satisfaction, I saw there was a big piece of adhesive covering most of his nose.

I didn't realize that Mr. Gold had slipped up beside me until he said, softly, "That's one from the other night, isn't it? With that <u>shlekht</u> (I think I spelled that right) 'aliens' sign?"

"Yeah. It's the one you conked."

"Apparently, not hard <u>enough</u>," he said. Then he shook his head. "This has happened before. The police I call, but they tell me as long as it's peaceful, they can't be arrested." He waved a hand toward the window. "I suppose they would call this peaceful."

At that point, as I looked out at the protestors, gathered there with their hateful placards and cruel faces, I couldn't have told you whether the escalating tension inside me was the seventh sense or my blood beginning to boil.

"Not for very much longer," I said.

"What?"

I turned to him. "Call the police, Mr. Gold. Tell them to get here as quickly as they can — the Bund has jumped one of your customers, and there may be a riot."

As I turned to go, he put a hand on my shoulder, gripping hard. I stopped and looked back into his concerned eyes.

"No, Mr. Brown," he said. "This is not your fight."

"It <u>is</u> my fight," I returned, so loud that the customers stared at me. "And it's every right-thinking American's fight!" I took a breath to calm myself down. "What happened in Germany isn't going to happen here. Now you get on that phone!"

With that, I headed out the door, right into the path of the protestors. Stopping in the doorway to zip up my CCC jacket — it might help cushion some blows if things got that far — I grabbed the first Bundist I ran into. He was a short young guy with a big nose, and I grabbed two fistfuls of the collar of a shirt that was two sizes too small for him. Jamming my nose against his, I growled, "Get out of here now, you maggot, before you get <u>mashed</u>!"

He squealed like a piglet. Dropping his sign, he jerked away from me and took off across the street, where a crowd had gathered to watch the protestors. Then, looking around at the others, I shouted, "You scum had better beat it! The cops are on the way!"

There was some muttering then, and one of 'em said, "We ain't doing any harm. We have the right to be here and not be harassed!"

"So does the proprietor of this store," I said. "Now, take off!"

Then, another voice, from behind me. "Oh.So the Jew lover returns!"

I whirled around and, sure enough, it was Elrich himself, bandaged nose and all, pushing his way through the others.

"Now, pally," he said, rolling up his sleeves as he walked, "I get to even things — with no old kike to sneak up and conk me when I'm not looking."

Suddenly, he swung a roundhouse right that would've put me on the pavement if it had connected. But, as bullies will do, he'd telegraphed the punch enough that I was able to back-step and put a hard right into his big belly.

And the fight was on. I knew this time not to underestimate him, that the lard he toted around on his frame was deceptive.So I played it smart. I knew I could move faster, and I did, ducking most of his punches and landing quite a few of my own.

I don't know how long this went on, up and down the sidewalk, but it seemed like hours. We seemed to be the only two figures moving; a tableau of background faces looking motionlessly on as we feinted and hit and backpedaled and attacked.

Then, I got a good one in, right in the middle of the patch on his nose. He yowled and grabbed his face, and as he crumpled to the sidewalk, I felt a hard blow to the back of my head. Then another.

The tableau had dissolved, and Elrich's buddies were whacking me with their signs and the sticks that held them up. They fell on me like red ants on a grasshopper, and I swung again and again, connecting as often as I missed.

But their sheer weight was forcing me down, and I knew that once I was laid out on the sidewalk, all of those bastards would dog pile me.

<u>Where are the coppers</u>? I wondered as the Bundists closed ranks around me, pummeling me with fists and sticks and signs. And then the terrible thought went through my head that Mr. Gold, not wanting trouble, might not have called the fuzz at all — and, to tell you the

truth, that notion sent a sick thrill of fear through me, a counterpoint to the blows hitting me from all sides.

I'd been beaten all the way down to the sidewalk when I heard the banshee wail of a police siren, through a wall of humanity that suddenly got a lot less dense. I looked up to see the little Nazis fleeing, leaving a clutter of signs in their wake. They'd abandoned their pal Elrich, who was attempting to rise and join them but was apparently still woozy from the last blow I'd given him.

Before I knew it, two officers were helping me up, while a third was cuffing Elrich, who wasn't putting up much of a fuss. I was a little groggy myself, but better off than _he_ was.

"You all right, son?" asked one of the cops.

"Sure," I said.

Just then, Mr. Gold entered the scene, which had suddenly become crowded with onlookers.

"This man was just trying to shop, Sergeant Feinstein, when these Bund members jumped him," Mr. Gold said, not bothering to explain how I could've been shopping outside his store on the sidewalk. He handed me a couple of parcels with my purchases in them. "The jackets will be ready next week," he said.

With a nod of his head, the sergeant indicated the bloody-faced Elrich, who was doing his best to sneer at me. "You want to sign a formal complaint against this bird?" he asked.

I sneered back at Elrich. "You bet your sweet . . . arm I do, Sergeant. And gladly."

He nodded, and ushered me into a patrol car, while the other two cops shoved Elrich in another.

"What's your name, son?" he asked on our way to headquarters.

I told him, adding, "Am I in trouble?"

"Hell, no. If I had _my_ way, you'd get a medal." He paused a moment. "You Jewish, by any chance?"

"No sir. But I _am_ anti-Nazi."

He nodded, and I thought I saw a quick smile.

It took a couple of hours to do the paperwork that put Elrich behind bars, and then Sergeant Feinstein offered to drive me back to my new digs. He wasn't a particularly talkative guy, but he did tell me that the Bund was "an annoyance, like mosquitos," especially because they knew what they could do and not do to keep from being arrested.

When we pulled up in front of the boarding house, Mrs. Dean met the police car before I had even gotten out.

"Oh, Lordy, Mr. Brown," she said. "Did I make a mistake? Are you some sort of criminal?"

Before I could say anything, the sergeant spoke. "No, ma'am. He just had an unfortunate run-in with some Nazis downtown." Then, he gave her a brief rundown of what had happened outside Gold's store, making me look more heroic than necessary.

"So," Sergeant Feinstein concluded, "if it were me, I'd be pretty proud of him."

"Oh, I am," she said. "C'm'on, Mr. Brown, and let's get you cleaned up."

I waved goodbye to the sergeant and walked with her to the door of her place, hurting but happy to be home and pleased with what had happened to Elrich and his pretend-Nazi pals. She walked me up to the bathroom, past three guys standing around the dining room table whom I figured were my fellow boarders. Once she'd patched me up, treated a few small open wounds with silver nitrate powder, and given me a couple of aspirins, I went down-stairs to that same table, which was piled with cold cuts with a big loaf of freshly baked bread, sliced thick, and a bowl of potato salad full of mustard and green olives, just the way I like it. I sat down, feeling the eyes of the other three tenants on me, but when Mrs. Dean gave them an abbre-viated version of what Sergeant Feinstein had told her, emphasizing that I'd been in a fight with anti-American Nazis, they all avowed that they didn't like heinies them-selves, shook my hand, and turned back to slapping sandwiches together and spooning out potato salad.

Scrawny people seem to be the rule in that

household. In addition to Mrs. Dean, there's a tall blond geek named Clyde Meadows, who says he's in charge of sporting goods at Garfinckel's, one of the biggest department stores in town. And Nicholas — Nick — Ubraski, another beanpole, with dark hair and complexion, is another one. He's older than the rest of us by a good seven or eight years and an accountant with the Treasury Department.

The odd guy out is a little butterball named James Keaton. Everyone calls him "Buster," of course, and I guess it's not surprising that he's the one I really hit it off with. We're not only just about exactly the same age, but we also share the same taste in literature — pulp magazines. I found this out at the table over our cold supper, when Clyde professed a fondness for Westerns and Nick for the book-of-the-month club offerings — he's a subscriber, and he volunteered to lend me any I might want.

"They'll help your intellect, Mr. Brown," he said, in sort of a stuffy fashion. "Good literature is like a good meal."

"Well," said Buster, spreading mustard all over his second or third sandwich, "give me baloney, and give me pulps," leading to an observation by Clyde.

"Buster, you're <u>already</u> full of baloney," he said, prompting good laughs from us all, even Mrs. Dean.

About halfway through the meal, a curious

little buzz began running through me — a kind of junior-grade version of the seventh sense, I guess. About the same time, I noticed some movement in the living room. When I turned to look, I saw in the half-darkness a middle-aged Oriental, dressed in work clothes, quietly running a carpet sweeper across the floor.

Following my gaze, Mrs. Dean said, "That's Mr. Saki. He's Japanese. Come to work here as a kind of handyman about six months ago. He can do about anything. Lives out back in a little shack I fixed up for him."

At the mention of his name, I saw the man look up from his work, and I put my napkin on the table and crossed the room toward him. Over my shoulder, I heard Mrs. Dean shout, "New boarder, Mr. Saki."

He bowed, and I stuck out my hand. "It's a pleasure to know you, sir," I said. The buzzing was louder now inside me, like the sound of agitated bees, but, oddly enough, not particularly unpleasant.

Taking my hand, he bowed again, saying, "You do me an honor."

I bowed back and returned to my dinner, the buzz subsiding. Mr. Saki went back to his work, and, later on, after everyone had finished eating, Buster and I stayed at the table and compared notes on our favorite pulps and pulp characters. His top-notch publishing house was Street & Smith, while mine was Popular, so we adjourned to our separate rooms and dug out copies of the magazines to lend one another. He seemed especially jazzed about <u>Crime Busters</u>, which I didn't know a lot about, and I was surprised that he'd never read an <u>Operator No. 5</u>.So we swapped, and I went to sleep that night reading about the exploits of the Keyhole, a newspaper columnist devoted to helping the poor and downtrodden, and a female private dick named Carrie Cashen.

Given what I'd been through that afternoon, I couldn't help but feel a kinship to those characters, and to Crime Busters everywhere — as well as a little bit of wonder about why Mr. Saki had triggered a little spell of seventh sense.

Your faithful two-fisted correspondent,
Robert

October 10, 1939
Tuesday evening

Dear John,

    Well, I made good on my threat to call in sick Monday morning, even though I felt a little guilty about the goldbricking. But, honestly, I wasn't really lying (although I admit to maybe pushing the sick-boy voice a little when I got Mr. Fletcher on the horn Monday morning); given everything that had happened, including the pummeling from Elrich and his Fascist chums, I was <u>beat</u> (no pun intended).

    Also, as you may remember, old Fletch already thought I had what my uncle Rich used to call "the running blues," so it wasn't such a hard sell. Fletcher appears to be plenty bullish on the benefits of paregoric. He even offered to bring me a bottle. I told him thanks, I had some, and I was going to take a big dose and go to bed.

    Which I did, minus the paregoric.

    You'll recall that I spent a lot of Sunday at the typer, laying everything out for you — and for me, I guess. Apparently I was going on pure adrenaline then, and if that was the case, it ran out about 7 p.m. Hell, all of a sudden I couldn't even hold my head up. I barely was able to undress before I hit the mattress, and I can't tell you much of anything that happened after that until breakfast. I was still as logy as a three-toed sloth when I descended the stairs. I bantered with the boys the best I could until around 7:30, then excused myself, went to the telephone nook, and rang up Mr. Fletcher (see above). Returning to the table, I told Mrs. Dean I'd just gotten the day off so I could rest up some more. She was sympathetic, and my fellow boarders didn't even razz me about it.

Maybe I limped just a little bit more than I needed to as I got up from the table and shambled off to my room, in the hopes that all of them would give me plenty of privacy. Once again, I didn't have to do much pretending. It was like Sunday evening all over again; I felt again like every last bit of energy was draining out of me like oil from a busted crankcase.

As things turned out, I got what I wanted, all right. Buster, Nick, and Clyde ankled the place without disturbing me a bit, and Mrs. Dean didn't even come in and wake me that afternoon, even after she took a telephone call for me.

It turned out to be important, but of course I didn't know that as I lay wrapped in the arms of Morpheus, a circumstance that lasted for a good seven hours. It wasn't until I roused myself for dinner, threw on a shirt and slacks, and headed downstairs to the common table that she stopped me.

"You had a call a couple of hours ago, Mr. Brown," she said, balancing a bowl of mashed potatoes in one hand and a platter of meat loaf in the other. "I wrote the number down on the pad in the nook." Beyond her, I saw Buster, Clyde, and Nick, already home from work and waiting at the table.

"Thanks," I said, and headed for the little first-floor cubbyhole that held the 'phone. Recognizing the number, I dialed it, waited through a half-dozen rings, and was just about to hang up when I heard a "hello" from Gena.

"Robert here," I said. "You called?"

"Oh. Yes." She seemed a little breathless. "Sorry to take so long to answer, but I was in the shower."

Imagining how she looked in the shower made for a nice mental exercise, believe me. I almost didn't hear her next words. But I would've known they were important, because suddenly, that familiar old skittering started inside me, as I heard her say, "What we talked about the other night — you know?"

"Sure."

"I think I need your help now."

Well, John, that statement kicked my seventh sense into high gear.

"I'm on my way."

"Thank you. You may want to hurry."

Was it my imagination, or did her voice

sound a little distorted, a little — <u>unnatural</u>?

"Hang on, Gena. Just hang on."

I cut off her call and put one in to Smokey Stover's dispatcher. Luckily, Smokey was on duty that day, and the man on the other end of the line said Smokey would be pulling up in about five minutes. That gave me just enough time, I thought.

I'd given a little thought to lycanthropes before drifting off to sleep, and I'd realized this situation wasn't much different from some of what I'd dealt with back in Mackaville. Were-animals are were-animals, no matter what kind they are, and I knew what would stop them. I also thought I knew how to deal with Gena, should she already be infected — a good likelihood, I thought, after talking to her on the 'phone.

So, bounding up to the second floor, I stopped in front of the bathroom medicine cabinet and grabbed the little bottle of silver nitrate powder Mrs. Dean had put around my Bund-induced wounds on Saturday evening, following the melee. Then I continued to my room. I took the old Colt and holster from underneath the clothes in my chest of drawers and put it in my briefcase. It was loaded, I knew, with those hollow-point bullets full of silver shavings that I'd made — and used — in Mackaville. I wished again there was some way to carry it on my person without attracting attention, but it was just too damn big.

Shrugging on a jacket, I headed out, ignoring the looks of my fellow boarders as I sped past them to the street, where Smokey Stover and his rumbling chariot already waited.

"You remember where you let the young lady off a couple of nights ago?" I asked as I climbed in the back.

"Chief, it's etched in my mind," he returned, winking. Then, sizing up the little nicks and bruises on my face, he added, "She didn't do <u>that</u> to you, did she?"

I grinned, even though it still hurt a little, and rubbed at a little bandage Mrs. Dean had put on my chin.

"Nope. Got into it again with some more damn Nazis."

Smokey shook his head. "You're a regular magnet for them boys, ain'tcha?"

"Sure looks that way," I agreed, taking a quick look at my battered visage in his rear-view mirror. "But I'd rather be a magnet for that young lady. So let's go."

"We're practically there," he said, jamming gears. Like a jackrabbit, the Checker cab jumped from the curb and headed down the street.

As we joined the rest of the traffic, I slipped the vial of silver nitrate out of my jacket pocket and held it up to the fading light, hoping there was enough there for what

I thought I might have to do. I was all jumpy inside, with the seventh sense really beginning to kick around, but my mind was clear enough. If Gena needed what I suspected she needed, I was ready.

Then, I saw Smokey's narrowed eyes in the mirror above his dashboard, looking back at me.

"Hey, chief," he said sternly. "You ain't planning to give that gal a Mickey Finn, are you?"

"No, Smokey. Of course not."

"Then what's that powder you got there?"

I gave him the best grin I could muster. "Bicarb," I said. "She's got rich tastes in food, and I'm trying to see if I've got enough to cover it."

"Oh."

"Don't want to burp in front of her like some backwoods rube, but it's better than getting a bellyache."

He nodded, his eyes flickering back to the road. "Sorry to suspect you. But I don't like being involved in nothing shady or under-handed, especially when it involves a good-looking young lady. She's got _class_, chief."

"Don't I know it," I returned, slipping the vial back in my pocket. I was suddenly deeply glad that he couldn't see inside my briefcase. It wouldn't have been quite as easy to explain away that hog leg pistol.

By the time we pulled up to Gena's apart-ment building, the seventh sense was knocking around inside me so hard I was almost shaking. When I handed Smokey the customary fin though his driver's-side window, he thanked me and said, "Want me to stick around, chief?"

It was hard to think with all those alarm bells going through me, but I did some quick figuring and said, "Give me an hour. If I'm not out here then, you can go on."

He looked me up and down, breaking into a grin. "An <u>hour</u>, huh? Okey-doke." Then, giving a long whistle, he pulled out into the gathering darkness.

Briefcase in hand, I made the foyer and looked until I spotted her last name above the buzzer for No. 324. Right after I pressed it there was a return buzz, clicking open the door to the small lobby, which, thankfully, was unoccupied when I slipped in and headed to the stairs. I was being especially furtive, and I wasn't sure why, but I knew enough to follow wherever my seventh sense — now ringing like a fire alarm — might be guiding me. Outside her door, I opened the briefcase, took out that old Peacemaker, and stuck it in my belt, under the jacket. The bulge it made was very noticeable, but I couldn't worry about that now.

I could hear her in there, moving around, and I started to knock. Then I changed my mind. Putting my mouth to the keyhole, I said, softly, "Gena."

The movement stopped.

"Gena," I said again. "It's Robert."

"Robert?" The voice was strained, agonized. "Robbbberttt?" It trailed off into something that was almost like a growl, and the door opened — onto something that was not quite Gena.

She was nude, but nude like an animal is nude, as though that were her normal state. She gave the impression, in that moment, of being covered in fur! Her apartment was dim, no light to speak of behind her, so maybe there wasn't any fact to that observation. I don't know. I do know that she almost jumped back at the sight of me, with a sharp hissing intake of breath, and even in that simple movement I saw that her feline grace had transmogrified into the movements of a real cat. Her blonde hair was a mane, her eyes wide and pulsating, her hands raised like claws.

The sight of her, half-human, half-beast, sent a sick thrill coursing through me, tripping the switches on my seventh sense. I knew then as surely as I've ever known anything that a battle was raging inside her — and the animal part of her was winning.

I had the revolver out, and I held it on her.

"This gun is loaded with silver bullets, Gena, any one of which will kill you," I said. "Do you understand?"

Her eyes flickered from the Colt to my face as the words hung in the air between us, my seventh sense vibrating behind them, around them, around Gena. A strange strangling sound came from deep in her throat.

"I can help you, Gena, but if you attack me, I'll kill you," I said softly. "I know you're fighting it inside. Fight harder. You can do it. Become a woman again, and I'll rid you of this."

The noise she was making escalated to a growl, her flashing eyes rolled in her head, and she flexed the fingers that looked now like claws. For a tense moment I was sure I was going to have to shoot her. But then, as though from a mighty effort, her features suddenly softened and her hands dropped to her sides. The fur I'd seen, or <u>thought</u> I'd seen, covering her body <u>evaporated</u> — that's the best word I can find to describe what happened. And suddenly, she was standing in front of me, as naked as the day she was born. How much was "real" and how much had I seen, supernaturally, in my mind's eye? I'll never know.

I do know that one of the reasons I knew she was a woman again is that she blushed all the way to her delectable bared breasts and ducked inside the door. By the time I'd followed her in, she'd grabbed up a bath towel that had been draped across the back of her sofa and was tucking it in around her.

I came inside with the briefcase, sticking the pistol back in my belt and shutting the door. Tears suddenly flowed from her eyes,

down her still-blushing cheeks, but she made
no sound.

"It's all right now, Gena," I said. "Keep
fighting, and we'll get you fixed up."

She swallowed. "Maybe . . ."

"Maybe what?"

Her eyes were wide and luminous. "Maybe
you should kill me."

"That won't be necessary, Gena," I told
her. "I can save you without killing you. But
it may hurt a little. Are you willing?"

She grabbed my hand then. "Oh God, yes,"
she said. "But how — ?"

And then, she seemed to see my banged-up
face for the first time.

"Robert — what's happened to you?"

I shook my head. "I'll tell you about it
later. Right now, it's not important. Sit
down, please."

As she eased herself into an overstuffed
chair, her eyes intent on me, I said, "Look,
Gena, a lot of us are not just what shows on
the surface. Your boyfriend is a good example. I'm sure he's responsible for what
you've become."

"Yes, I think so. He's — he's not human.
It wasn't <u>him</u> who did this to you?"

"No. But he could do much worse to us
both. I knew it the first time he and I saw
one another. Don't ask me how I know this,
but I do, and I've dealt with it before. He's
a lycanthrope, a changeling. A person who's
part animal."

She shook her head slowly, looking at the floor. "Yes. Maybe . . . I think you're right. He's made me into something that frightens me. After I left him last night, I had horrible nightmares, terrible dreams about — about killing. About tearing into people with my teeth and <u>eating</u> them. <u>Chil-dren</u>. And I was <u>enjoying</u> it. <u>Craving</u> it.

"I — when I awoke, late in the morning, the nightmares were still clinging to me. I've stayed right here in my apartment all day long, because I'm afraid to go out. But something seems to be <u>tugging</u> at me, demanding that I leave here and do . . . what I was doing in the dreams. I fight it, and it goes away for a short while, but soon it's back again."

She swallowed. "Nothing's helped. I've taken cold showers. I've tried to read a book and listen to the radio. But my mind is fogged with all of those ugly, terrible images, and I can't shake them. I'm being, I don't know — <u>compelled</u> to make them real. That's why I finally called you."

"I told you I could help you, Gena," I said.

She looked up. "You can?"

"I can. Because I'm a warlock."

"An oar lock?" Confusion spread across her features. "What do you mean? How can an oar lock help me?"

A laugh exploded out of me; I couldn't help it. Her eyes darkened, and quickly I told her, "No, Gena. Not <u>oar</u> — <u>war</u>. A warlock is a male witch. I hinted this to you the other night at dinner, but here it is without any sugar coating: I can do magic, and this magic can break whatever he's done to you. Do you believe me?"

She nodded, slowly.

"Good." I looked around the apartment into her kitchen, where a coffee pot sat in the stove.

"Any coffee left in that pot?"

"A little," she said. "But it's from this morning."

"Pour a cup of it and bring it back in here. Bring a spoon with it. Then I'll have a few questions I'll need you to answer."

"All right." She got up and walked to the kitchen like a person in a dream. My seventh sense was still raging, but a kind of righteous feeling had come over it — hard to explain, but there it was, and I think it was telling me I was on the right path. It was a good thing, too, as I was on new ground here, trying to remember everything I could from my years-long study of magic and the occult.

I was also trying not to be distracted by the movements of her body underneath that short white terrycloth towel.

Coffee cup cradled in both hands, she sat back down and looked up at me like a sad child.

"I apologize in advance for being so personal, Gena," I said, "but there are certain questions you're going to have to answer. The first one is very important. Has Fehring ever bitten you hard enough to draw blood?"

Her face flushed again then, her eyes flickering down to the cup of cold coffee. "No. No. Last night, he did come close." She looked back up, craning her neck a bit so that I could see a dark hickie near her shoulder blade.

"Have you had sexual relations with him?"

That question caused another reddening of her face, another glance away. "Not in the accepted sense, no. I've <u>satisfied</u> him in other ways, but I'm not, I don't — I'm terribly afraid of having a baby."

"Again, Gena, I'm not trying to be prurient, but this is also extremely important. When he kisses you, are they — well, <u>slobbery</u>, for lack of a better word."

This time, she didn't blush. "Oh, yes," she said. "He's a very <u>messy</u> kisser. But what could that possibly have to do with anything?"

I took a deep breath, knowing that she had to believe what I was going to tell her next, and wondering if she would. "It's where you've gotten that animalistic nature you've been fighting, both in your dreams and in your waking hours today. Your pal Fehring can infect others with his bite. He hasn't bitten you, but his saliva has been enough to start bringing out the animal in you. And I know it's gotten worse with every petting session you've had."

I watched her face closely, hoping to see understanding and acceptance. After a few moments, her eyes widened, and she seemed almost startled.

"Oh, my Lord, yes," she said. "I see it now. I understand some of the things he's said to me, about our 'love' lasting through the ages, about —" Stopping herself, she added, "Do you really think you can cure me?"

"Yes. You and I can whip it." I pulled out the ottoman in front the overstuffed chair and sat down, facing her. "I believe you have a partial infection from his saliva. If we can neutralize that, you should be all right. But you must trust me and do what I say."

For the first time, she smiled. "You're the boss," she said.

Reaching over, I took the coffee cup from her hands, produced the little vial of silver nitrate powder out of my jacket, and shook a small portion into her cup, stirring it around with the spoon. It had to be enough to do what I hoped it would do, but not too much — I knew ingesting too much of it could cause respiratory problems and other bad things. The last thing I wanted was for the cure to be as bad as the illness.

"I have to admit that I suspected a situation like this when you called, so I came prepared." I stirred a bit more and then continued. "Now, when it's your time of the month, do you ever have bad cramps?"

Of course, the blush returned, almost scarlet this time. "You're certainly being _intimate_ this evening," she said.

"It's important."

"Well, yes, I do."

"What I'm going to give you will make you feel like that. You're going to have some king — or queen — sized cramps, but they shouldn't last very long. After that, you should be free from the infection and the nightmares. Are you willing?"

Without a word, she took the cup and drank it down in two gulps, shaking her head and grimacing at the taste of it. I knew it wasn't pleasant, but she downed it like a real trouper.

Then, suddenly, she gasped, and the cup and saucer clattered to the carpet.

"My God!" She almost shouted, bending forward in pain. "You've poisoned me!"

I put a hand on her bare shoulder, steadying her. "No. Stay with it. It'll be over soon."

With a noise somewhere between a scream and a moan, she slid from my grasp to the floor, actually writhing in pain. Then she snarled, growled, and was on her feet, the towel dropping from her body, her face once again taking on the features of a cat, her hands turning clawlike. Like a jungle animal, she sprang from the floor as I stepped back, my hand on the Colt in my belt.

Then she vomited all over the carpet and sprawled forward, hitting the floor like a sack of flour.

I watched as she lay there for a few moments, groaning, and then helped her up. There was no sign of the animal in her now. She was soft in my hands as I rearranged the towel around her.

I'd done it, by damn. The silver had killed whatever Fehring had planted in her, and it would stay in her bloodstream. Maybe it wouldn't have worked if he'd bitten her, but my cure had been enough for whatever she'd had to face.

I'd be lying if I didn't tell you I was pretty proud of myself. And even though we had to clean up a mess and she had to take another shower — and amazingly, after all she'd been through, remember to daub on some more Shalimar — we still made it downstairs in time to be at the curb when Smokey Stover pulled up in his taxi. Since we were both suddenly famished and also had plans to make, we agreed that dinner would be a good idea.

On our way to the Mayfair, I asked how she'd known to call me at the boarding house, and she nodded toward Smokey, who was pretending not to listen.

"You don't think you're the only one who has one of his cards," Gena said with a smile. "He made sure I got one the other night. And between his dispatcher and him, I located you fairly quickly."

"Very glad you did," I told her.

She nodded, taking my arm and looking into my eyes.

"Me, too," she said.

I'll tell you all about those plans in my next letter.

Your pal and faithful correspondent,
Robert

October 12, 1939
Thursday evening

Dear John,

    After all the <u>War and Peace</u>-length
missives you've been receiving from me
lately, this one will probably seem as short
as the back of a picture postcard. It's
because not much more has happened in the
past couple of days — although I have a
feeling that's going to be changing sooner
rather than later.

    Right now, though, I'll just cut to the
chase. When we last left our hero and his
beautiful blonde companion, they were headed
for the Mayfair supper club, following a
harrowing ordeal that thankfully had come out
all right for 'em both. This time, they were
waited on by a pretty girl in South Sea garb.
I think she was supposed to be from Bali or
Bora Bora — someplace like that. They got
another couple of zombies, which he figured
might help the girl forget about what he'd
put her through a couple of hours earlier,
and when it came time to order, he got the
filet mignon, with sauteed mushrooms, but she
just ordered a molded mayonnaise salad.

    "To tell you the truth," Gena said, after
the island girl had taken our orders back to
the kitchen, "the thought of eating meat

right now makes me kind of sick to my stomach."

I told her I wasn't surprised, considering what she'd been through, as the sight of her wolfing down (yes, I know) a nearly bloody piece of steak the last time we'd visited the Mayfair flashed through my mind. Surely, her gusto for that steak was all wrapped up with Fehring and his attempts to escort her into an unending darkness.

But, thankfully, that all now seemed to be water under the bridge. On the other hand, I knew he would try to see her again, and I wasn't sure what he'd do once he realized that she had escaped his dominance.

So, I let her take a couple of good pulls on her zombie before I said, as offhandedly as I could, "You know you can't ever see Fehring again, don't you?"

She nodded, not looking at me, taking another sip through the paper straw. At that moment, she looked like a beautiful young kid in a soda parlor.

"Are you going to be able to do that? Stay away from him, I mean?"

She looked up at me then. Her eyes were troubled.

"I think so," she said. "But Robert, I don't know. I feel that his spell over me is broken — that you broke it for me. Still, his eyes. They have a power in them. You know that."

"And _you_ know it's an evil power."

"Yes."

I took a sip of my own zombie. Maybe it was the events of the past few hours — or, hell, the past few _days_ — but I felt an almost physical release as the alcohol warmed me. I told myself I'd better be careful, remembering I'd heard somewhere that drunkenness was four-fifths psychological.

"Okay." I exhaled. "When's the next time you're supposed to see him?"

"Tomorrow. He'll be at Woodies when I clock out at six p.m. He wants to take me out on the town, he said."

I considered that for a moment. "Well," I said finally, "instead of going out on the town, I think you'd better go _out_ of town. Immediately, and for at least a few days. Can you do that?"

"You mean leave?"

"Exactly. And before Friday evening."

I thought this might fluster her a little, but she remained calm, growing thoughtful.

"It's possible," she said. "Mrs. Stefanic, my supervisor, can be a pretty soft touch, especially if a girl has a family emergency."

"Could you have one?" I asked.

"I'd have to stretch the truth a little," she returned. "My mother and father are both healthy as horses, knock on wood. But I couldn't be gone long. You remember when we came here before and talked about how we both had to go to work, right out of school?"

"Sure."

"Well, what I didn't tell you was that my job at Woodies doesn't just support _me_. I'm sending everything I can spare back to my folks, and they need it. My dad had a dairy back before the crash; he lost it a couple of years ago. He gets work wherever and whenever he can, but there've been some dry stretches lately. Mom's managed to scrape up a little income, working at a little notions store part-time. But I'm not sure they could get along without my income for very long at all."

She stopped as our South Sea waitress brought our food, setting Gena's gelatinous white salad down first. It wiggled a bit, almost like something alive. She looked at it, then up at me, and shook the plate a little, laughing as she watched her entree shimmy. I laughed right back. It felt good.

Meanwhile, a plan had formed in my mind. I guess it had been percolating for a while, because I knew she couldn't stay away from D.C. — or Fehring — forever. If she stayed in Milwaukee, there were no guarantees that he couldn't ultimately track her down if he wanted to. Plus, she would lose her job at the store, and that would bring on a whole new group of problems.

I knew there was only one thing to do.

And John, tomorrow night I'm going to do it.

Your pal and faithful correspondent,
Robert

October 15, 1939
Sunday afternoon

Dear John,

Remember that letter I sent you a couple of days ago, and how I joked about how short it was?

This one will not be. Short, I mean. It's going to take a little time and a ton of typing to give you the lowdown on the situation I found myself thrown into on Friday evening.

To be honest, I threw _myself_ into it, so I've got no one to blame but me. And while it worked out all right, it wasn't quite the conclusion I would've wished for.

So, here goes:

First of all, after our Monday evening dinner, I shared with Gena my idea regarding what to do about her and Fehring, and while she initially protested my getting deeply involved, I managed to allay her fears. I think knowing that I'd cured her of her lycanthropic tendencies did the trick for her; I essentially convinced her I could do something like that with her (now) ex-boyfriend. I didn't say that the stakes were significantly higher — that either Fehring or I might die as a result — but maybe I didn't have to.

Smokey ferried us back to her apartment, but I exited his chariot a couple of blocks away, just in case Fehring or even some of the Bund goons might be hanging around the neighborhood. Smokey poked along after letting me off in order to give me a chance to reach Gena's building before he and she did, and I was crouched there in the shadows beside the concrete stairs when he pulled up to let her out. I watched and waited for about 10 minutes, and as nearly as I could tell, no one followed her, so I slipped in and joined her in her apartment.

We'd made plans for Smokey to return in an hour. By that time, I hoped, Gena would be packed and ready to sneak away from Fehring. As she threw things into a suitcase, I called the station and got the time for the next train leaving in the direction of Milwaukee.

We were in luck. There was one heading northwest at 11:18 — plenty of time for Gena to make it. And she did.

Of course, I couldn't have said for sure that she got away scot-free. But, blending into the background of the depot, which even at this time had plenty of people milling around in it, I kept a wary eye out until she'd boarded. I didn't even tell her goodbye or give her so much as a wave. If anyone was watching for us, I didn't want to telegraph my position. We'd worked it all out earlier.

I felt pretty good as I watched her train gather speed and roll out of the station. For one thing, I figured if she or I had been in any immediate danger, the seventh sense would've given me at least some warning. But after the incident at her apartment, my insides had been completely calm. And they stayed that way when good old faithful Smokey, who'd stuck around to make sure everything was going to be all right, took me back to my room at Mrs. Dean's.

Yes, indeed, it had been one hell of a day.

The next morning, I made myself get up and head out to work a little early, just so I could stay in Mr. Fletcher's good graces after taking Monday off. It would be four full workdays before my plan to confront Fehring would go into action, and I only hoped those days would be peaceful. Lately, I'd been reminded once again that there's such a thing as too much excitement, and I'd just as soon be getting my thrills from the likes of the Spider or Operator No. 5 for a while.

Old Fletch was solicitous when I arrived, not long after 7 a.m. He and I were the only ones in the office then — I assume he goes home at some point, but he's never left before me, and he's always there when I show up. I knew he'd likely ask me something about my banged-up face, so I decided to tell him the truth, and kind of mix it in with my being sick.

Sure enough. His eyes widened when he saw

me and he muttered, "My goodness. What happened to you?"

"It was a one-two punch," I told him. "I got sick, and when I went out to get some paregoric, I was attacked by some Bund members."

Yes, I fibbed. But it made a better story, at least as far as Mr. Fletcher's concerned, and the untrue parts weren't all that important. I didn't want him to think I'd been out looking for a fight when I was supposed to be suffering from some sort of abdominal lockup.

Then I let him know how grateful I was he'd let me take Monday off to recuperate.

"I'm going to make it up to you, Mr. Fletcher," I told him. "I'll come in early and stay late the next few days, so that I can get everything back on track."

His eyes crinkled under his Moe Howard bangs, and he gave me a solicitous smile.

"If your health allows," he said, "that would be a nice gesture. It doesn't look as though your injuries are awfully serious, although I'm sure they're painful."

"I'll be all right," I said, sounding for all the world like Freddie Bartholomew in <u>Little Lord Fauntleroy</u>. Stiff upper lip and all of that.

"Good man," he said, actually patting me on the shoulder.

I guess Fletch does finally go home after a day of work, but he sure didn't light a shuck Tuesday night — or, for that matter,

Wednesday or Thursday. I worked until nearly 8 p.m. all three of those days, and he was there in his office for me to tell him goodbye every time.

I don't know if I've given you a description of my work environment or not. To sketch it briefly: It's a big open area inside a building, with about 20 desks spaced out at intervals under a low ceiling and a person at each one, most of them doing the same things I do — typing orders and other documents for the U.S. government. The clattering of typewriter keys never lets up; it's like background music in a movie. There are a couple of guys here, and uniformed officers from the various branches are always coming through, waving papers and doing their best to look important, but most of the workers around me are women of varying ages. Maybe a half-dozen of 'em are real lookers, but most of those work in another part of the compound, so I haven't met them yet. Mr. Fletcher is the immediate supervisor over all of us.

My mildly damaged face drew several long stares on Tuesday, but the only person besides Fletch making any comment was an older woman who works about five desks down and two back from me. I was tapping away on some assignment or other when she came by and introduced herself as Leah Friedman.

"I'm sorry about your face, Mr. Brown," she said softly. "But I want you to know I appreciate what you did. Thank you." Then she was gone. I was pretty certain she was Jewish, and I wondered if she and Mr. Gold knew one another, or if she'd just been grateful that I'd taken on some Nazis. At any rate, she knew how I'd gotten my battle scars — such as they are.

Then there was Mrs. Dean, God bless her. On those three nights, when I got in around 9 p.m. or later, she always had a cold meat loaf sandwich waiting in the ice box for me. Mrs. Dean's meat loaf may not be the best in town, but it's mighty welcome when you're as hungry as I was after all that extra work — and my usual Coca-Cola lunches.

Tuesday, after she brought out the sandwich and a big glass of milk from the cold closet, she told me I'd had a call from "a young lady."

"She didn't give her name, and she didn't give me a number," Mrs. Dean said. "But it sounded far away. I think it was a long distance call." Her eyes narrowed a little, and she smiled. "Can't say for sure, but it sounded like it might be that same girl who called you the other day."

I'm sure she was angling for more info, but I played dumb and just nodded.

"She was polite enough, though," continued Mrs. Dean. "Asked if I wouldn't mind giving you a message. 'Of course,' I told her."

I raised my eyebrows. "What did she want to tell me, Mrs. Dean?"

"She said she'd made it, and everything was fine."

"That's all?"

"That was it."

She held me in her gaze and smiled again — expectantly. It was obvious to me that she was craving the lowdown on my romantic life. At that moment, I decided there was no harm in telling her, although I may have stretched the truth a bit.

"Well," I said, aw-shucksing it like Gary Cooper, "don't tell the fellows, but I've got a girlfriend. She just left town to visit her folks, and she was calling to let me know she got there all right."

"That's thoughtful of her," Mrs. Dean said.

"It sure is. She's a thoughtful girl."

Ms. Dean nodded, still smiling, and then excused herself and began puttering around the kitchen. I finished my sandwich and, finally, got to my room. I was so tired I didn't even pick up the copy of the latest _Spider_, which lay on the stand next to my bed — and, brother, you know me, and you know I must've been fagged out if I couldn't even manage to read a chapter or two of my favorite pulp.

On Thursday, I really turned to and got a lot done, typing with one hand and wiping sweat with the other, as we used to say in the CCC. I left at 7 p.m., which had been my plan all along. Earlier that day, during the noon hour, I'd called Smokey's dispatcher and asked if the cab could be waiting for me when I got off, and sure enough, it was sitting right there, engine idling, when I walked out the front door.

"Please tell me we're picking up your choice young quail again, chief," he said, by way of greeting. "It's been too long."

"She's still gone," I told him. "But I'd like for you to drive me to Woodies."

"Sure," he said, throwing the car into gear. "It ain't gonna be the same, though."

"Don't I know it," I returned.

It was nearly dark when we got to the Woodward & Lothrop building. I knew it wouldn't be open at this time of the evening, but I felt the need to scout it anyway.So while Smokey waited in his chariot, I got out and walked around the massive edifice, making a mental note about the location of the fire escapes. I remembered there were 10 stories to the place, so I figured the roof to be six floors above the counter where Gena worked.

The reconnoitering took longer than I thought. By the time Smokey dropped me off at Mrs. Dean's, it was coming up on 10 p.m. and the house was quiet. I had to use my key on the front door, and then I crept upstairs, not wanting to awaken anyone. When I got to my room, I found a note in my landlady's handwriting Scotch-taped to the door.

Your father called you on the telephone at 6:32 p.m., it read. _He would like for you to call him back at your earliest opportunity. Sincerely, Mrs. Dean._

Well, John, you remember that my old man goes to bed with the chickens. It was too late to give him a ring then, but I figured I could raise him early the next morning, before work. That was maybe my only option. I planned to be very busy after work Friday.

So, I set my alarm clock for 5:30, got to the bathroom before anyone else, and was at the Ameche by 6 a.m. It took only a minute or two to make the connection to Hallock, and then I heard Dad's voice on the other end, as the operator asked if he'd accept the charges for a collect call from Robert A. Brown.

"Yes," he said, and then, "Hi, son."

"Hello, Dad."

"Got your new address and phone number in the mail yesterday. Called to tell you about your Grandmother Frank."

Dad, as you know, is not only a man of few words, but he's been known to pinch pennies until Honest Abe squeals. I got the idea that he somehow thought the 'phone company was charging him by the word.

"What about her, Dad?"

"She's gonna die, son. Pretty soon now. Cancer. Don't guess you need to come back for the funeral, since I know it'd be tough for you to leave your job. But she wanted your address. So I gave it to her. I guess she's sending you something. Don't know what. Thought I ought to tell you, so you could be on the lookout for it."

"Thanks, Dad. And I'm sorry."

"She's lived a good life. I'll write when she goes."

"Thanks."

"You getting along o.k.?"

"Sure. Everything's going fine."

"Good. Your mother says hello, and don't forget to write."

"I won't."

"So long then," he said, and hung up.

Although it didn't surprise me about Grandma — she'd been going downhill for a couple of years — it was still a little bit of a shock to hear about her impending death. Even though we'd always called her Grandma Frank, it was really her maiden name. She was my father's mother. Like her son, she was a very reserved person, hard to know. But I still liked her a lot. I'd never known her husband, my paternal grandfather; he'd died a couple of years before I was born. He'd been a school administrator, but that's just about the extent of what I knew about him. Grandma Frank was not given to much ruminating about the past — at least, not in my presence.

After I shut off my light that night, lying in bed, I tried to imagine what she might be sending me, but those thoughts were continually crowded out by the overriding anxiousness about what I knew I had to do the next day.

It seems like it began thundering in the middle of the night, and the rain was splashing down Friday morning even before I got up — a perfect beginning for a Friday the 13th. The storm persisted throughout the day, ebbing and flowing, thunder crashing and lightning flashing outside the windows of the downtown office. Everybody was a little jumpy, and that certainly included me — even though my agitation didn't have a lot to do with the weather. A persistent dull seventh-sense rumbling had added to my unease. I'm no triskaidekaphobe, but the fact that it was indeed Friday the 13th wasn't exactly a tonic for my nerves, especially when I let my mind wander to what I was going to have to do that night.

All day long, as the rainwater sluiced down the windows, I tried to keep my mind on the orders I was typing, but they all seemed to run together, and it took some real effort not to bollix them up. I looked at the big clock on the wall a lot more than usual that day, and when 5 p.m. rolled around, I was the first one out the door. I don't think I even said goodbye to Mr. Fletcher.

I had no time to waste. I grabbed a

streetcar, ran through the rain the extra couple of blocks to the boarding house once it let me off, and got up the stairs in a hurry, grabbing up my jacket and briefcase. The latter, you might remember, held that old pistol I'd brought from Mackaville, the one that's too big to conceal adequately on my person. The last time I'd had it out, I'd pointed it at Gena. That seemed like ages ago.

I got ready so fast that I actually had to wait for Smokey and his cab. As I stood on Mrs. Dean's porch, clutching my case and peering out into the whipping rain, I heard someone shut the door behind me.

"Mr. Brown?"

It was Mrs. Dean.

I turned to her. "Yes, ma'am."

"You're not getting out in this awful weather?"

"I'm afraid so," I said, working up a smile. "More work to do."

She shook her head sadly. "I've got a nice meat loaf for dinner," she said.

Just then, I saw the gleam of Smokey's chariot, pulling to a stop at the curb in front. I broke toward it in a trot, rain pelting me, as I shouted back, "Thank you! If there's any left, I'd sure be glad to have a sandwich later!"

Then I was in the cab, headed toward Woodward & Lothrop — and who knows what.

I suppose it was the weather, but Smokey

was almost subdued. He didn't even ask about Gena, especially when I told him I wouldn't need him anymore once he dropped me off. The reason I didn't want him to stay around, I told myself, was because I wasn't at all sure what was going to happen or how long I was going to have to stay there to get the job done, and there was no sense in his being out in the storm any longer than necessary. But I realized it wasn't just that. It was also because I really didn't know how this was going to end, and if it ended badly, I knew he'd at least be spared if he wasn't around.

Although Smokey protested a little when I dismissed him in front of Woodies, he seemed grateful that I'd let him go. As I watched him drive away, I figured he was probably done for the evening and heading back to wherever he lived, where he'd pour himself a beer and maybe listen to Colonel Stoopnagle's quiz program.

At that moment, standing in the blowing rain, listening to the thunder rumble ominously, I wished fervently that I could join him.

Then I was in the store and onto the elevator, getting off at the fourth floor — Gena's floor — and finding a good place of concealment behind a rack of dresses next to the stairway exit. I checked my strap watch. It was 5:54, only a few minutes before closing time. Very soon, he'd be here.

My heart pounded and swirled in a mad

dance with the seventh sense jumping inside me, and when it became more furious, I knew he was on his way up.

Sure enough, the elevator door opened and Fehring suavely sauntered out, walking like he had a broomstick attached to his spine, heading toward the counter where Gena usually worked. Even though I was halfway across the vast room, I could see his body tighten with surprise when another young woman — this one a slim brunette I'd never seen before — came over to wait on him.

I let them talk for a moment, and then, suddenly, burst out of my hiding place.

"Hey! Fehring!" I shouted. "You want Gena, you'll have to get <u>me</u> first!"

And with that, I threw open the doorway to the stairs and tore upward, taking three steps at a time, briefcase swinging in my left hand. I had a decent head start, and I was in pretty good physical shape, but I still didn't know whether I could make it up those six sets of stairs before he overtook me.

Those few minutes of flight came in a blur, punctuated by my panting and gasping, as I zipped past the big numbers painted on the walls. Floor 6, 7, 8, 9, and then, suddenly, the stairs ended at a little building, not much bigger than a telephone booth — the "doghouse" entrance to the roof. I hauled ass through it and stepped out into the still-raging storm, just as a wicked flash of lightning exploded in the sky. Running across the combination of tar and metal, I dodged behind a metal ventilator and fumbled the pistol out of my briefcase.

Then, there was only the sound of the wind and the rain and the thunder. I carefully fastened the briefcase, set it down, and peered around the vent, Colt at the ready.

It seemed as though I waited forever, senses jangling. Then, I thought I saw movement near the doghouse booth.

The raging inside me matched the raging all around me. I kept my eyes on the little building, strained to listen through the noise of the storm. Then, something flashed around it, something darker than lightning. It happened so quickly that I wasn't sure it had happened at all.

Suddenly, a big flash lit up the ominous sky, a jarring crack of thunder right on its heels. I jumped and, even through the raging storm, heard the unmistakable sound of a laugh!

"Don't let the weather scare you," a voice half-shouted, half-hissed. "I am _far_ more deadly. And tonight, you shall die — not quickly, nor pleasantly."

Suddenly, the voice was on the other side of me, but much closer.

"You caused me to lose a willing convert — or, if the conversion didn't take, a tasty meal. Now, _you_ will be that meal."

Another bolt of lightning struck a vent on

that same side, with a great spray of sparks and a blast of staticky noise, followed by a snarl of surprise. I turned and ran hard in the opposite direction, toward the edge of the roof, hoping my memory was right about the location of the fire escape.

Behind me, through the machine-gun sound of the wind-whipped rain, I could make out the frenzied scrabbling of long nails on the roof, and worse, much worse, that rumbling hellish laughter. Suddenly, I understood that the storm was helping me. When the next bolt of lightning exploded, I could see a partial outline of the monster — enough to know that he was facing away from me. Because of the pelting rain and incessant peals of thunder, the thing couldn't hear me. Plus, all that rain was killing my scent!

As another thundering crash rolled over us, I kept going as quickly as I could across the roof, slamming my shins into endless sheet-metal vents as I tried to see my way through the storm. I knew if I made the fire-escape ladder and got down to the next land-ing, I'd be relatively safe. The silver-loaded slugs were still in my pistol, and if — _when_ — he came down the ladder after me he wouldn't be able to dodge my shots.

I'd almost made it to the edge of the roof when the thunder let up for a moment and I slid to a halt, dropping behind another of the air-conditioning vents. He heard me and turned, and, once again, I caught a glimpse of that huge wolf-like shape, bristling with black fur, dodging in and out of the structures that dotted the rooftop, running on all fours. Ducking down, I breathed as shallowly as I could, even as I watched him rear up, grab my now-empty briefcase, and hurl it into the dark sky with a long laugh. He dropped down again, disappearing from my sight.

Then, the voice again. Too close.

"I cannot see you yet, swine. But this storm will not last forever. And when it goes, _you_ go."

The laugh came again, shattered suddenly by a slash of blinding light not 50 feet from me.

That was when it hit me that the edge of the building was lined with what I had first thought were radio aerials. They weren't. They were lightning rods, and through the tumult, I silently gave thanks. They were drawing the storm _to_ us, making it easier for me to evade the thing that Fehring had become.

The subsequent explosion of thunder allowed me to make another 15 feet or so without the beast hearing me. When I slid again behind a ventilator, I spied a blur of motion to my right. He'd not seen me move, but he was still too close.

After each lightning strike, the rain seemed to intensify, and that helped, too. I was gasping by this time — all around me, the very air seemed electrified — and too late I realized that was all the noise it took for him to locate me. As the laugh began again, a large black shadow leaped in my direction.

John, I figured I was at the end of the trail. Sure, I had the pistol, but there was no guarantee I could get an accurate shot through the rain and the wind. The shadow loomed up — and then, I felt rather than saw the monster.

Before I could stop myself, I blasted off a couple of shots. At the time I had no way of knowing it, but the metal air vent beside me had amplified the gunfire and sent it booming down an air shaft into the store, causing a panic.

I figured that out later. But even if I'd known it at the time, I wouldn't have cared. Because at that instant, only 20 or 30 feet from me, a wolf as big as a pony, huge and shaggy, eyes burning green through the raging darkness, stood on all fours atop a shed-like structure, facing me and eyeing my pistol.

"Yes, bullets hurt," came that loud, hissing voice. "But they can't kill me, swine!"

With that, he gathered himself to spring forward. I jerked the six-gun up and got off three quick shots, but with the wind and the rain and the flashes and explosions going on all around me, I wasn't as accurate as I should've been. One did part his hair — or hell, _fur_ — before spattering on a metal shed behind him. Then, it did something I couldn't have expected. It ricocheted off that little corrugated metal building, the hollow-nosed lead slug disintegrated, and shreds of lead and silver spattered into the creature. It screamed like a woman, jumped to the floor of the rapidly flooding roof, and with super speed crawled behind that little shed — but not before it had suddenly changed from a four-legged wolf into a scurrying man without a stitch of clothing on his body.

The transformation, over in a twinkling, stunned me so much that I just stood there in the rain, the storm crashing all around me, while he raced to the doghouse booth and through, slamming the door behind him.

I followed, my feet sending up big splashes of rainwater as I ran to the little building — which was locked. I guess it was just as well. I don't think I could've shot a naked man. It just didn't seem right, somehow.

As I stood in the storm, pondering what to do next, I heard from ten stories below me the wail of sirens. Finding my way to the edge of the roof, I peered down through the relentless churning of the storm to see three police cars screeching to a halt in front of the main entrance. The storm seemed to be letting up a little now, and I knew I couldn't be caught on top of the building with a pistol, and I certainly wasn't going to leave it behind. That's when I remembered the echoing sounds of my first shots down the air vent and figured that was the reason for the cops — and another reason for me to beat a hasty retreat.

Well, my investigations of the day before paid off. I found my way to a fire escape and went down it like an ape, jumping rungs when I thought I could do it safely. I raced downward eight floors like I was trying to qualify for the Olympics, my hands and feet slipping on the wet metal, and finally hit the stairs that took me to the last platform. Sticking the Colt in the waistband of my pants, I paused, caught my breath, and slipped over, dropping the last 10 feet into the alley behind the store. As I hit the pavement, I heard another cop car racing past, siren blasting.

By this time, the storm had subsided, leaving behind a steady rain. I stood at the entrance to the alley, took a deep breath, covered up the pistol as best as I could with my jacket, and waltzed down the sidewalk, showing a lot more confidence than I felt. A few yards in front of me, a trolley was just starting to pull out, and I jumped on, settling on a seat in the back. I was conscious of eyes on me, and I knew I was dripping wet, but there wasn't anything I could do about it, so I just grinned when I caught anyone looking. Maybe the little nicks and bruises on my face made my fellow passengers wary of doing anything more than staring

at me. But no one said a word to me, and I
didn't offer any conversation either.

It was a very long, very damp, and very
round-about ride to the boarding house. By
the time I could see it in the now almost
gentle rain, the streetcar's heater had even
dried me out a little.

Believe it or not, the adventure wasn't
over — or, I guess I should say, I had
another surprise waiting when I got home.
I've worn myself to a nub telling you about
my rooftop encounter, so I'll save that for
the next letter. What I <u>will</u> say is that when
I got to my room, there was a big meat loaf
sandwich sitting on my end table. I've seldom
seen anything more welcome.

Your pal and faithful correspondent,
   Robert

October 16, 1939
Monday night (late)

Dear John,

    It's funny, but the first thing I did both
Saturday and Sunday was buy early editions of
the <u>Times-Herald</u> and the <u>Post</u> to see if my
dustup with Fehring's lupine alter-ego on the
Woodies roof had drawn any sort of notice
from the press. Once I got to thinking about
it, it seemed highly unlikely, though. Sure,
the cops had been summoned after someone
reported a gunshot — at least that's what I'm
assuming — but nobody had really seen
anything, except for me and my adversary. (Of
course, I'd seen <u>plenty</u>.)

    Maybe I was just thinking that, against
all odds, Fehring — as either himself or the
wolf — had been spotted trying to leave the
premises by one of the boys in blue and he'd
been captured. But no such luck. There wasn't
so much of a column inch about it in either
of the papers.

    But that's not why I'm writing you at this
late hour. Instead, I want to tell you about
the package that was waiting for me at the
boarding house when I got back from work this
evening. It was just inside the door, and
both Buster and Clyde were examining the
outside of the package and the tag that came

with it. When I opened the door, they looked up and grinned.

"Hey, Robert, look at what the Railway Express man just brought you," Buster said.

"Must be some pretty valuable stuff," added Clyde, running his fingers through his mop of blond hair. "Looks to me like it cost twelve simoleons to get it to you."

Bending down to look at the return address, I said, "Yeah. It's some family stuff from my old grandma. She's been real sick. In fact, she's probably dead by now."

That sobered them up.

"We're sorry," Clyde said. "We didn't know." Buster nodded as both of them made sympathetic faces.

"It's okay," I said. "We expected it." Hefting the box, which was heavier than it looked, I added, "I think I'll see what's inside. I'd invite you guys up to watch me get it open, but some of the stuff inside might be of a . . . _personal_ nature. You understand."

They both nodded. "Oh. Sure," said Buster. "We'll see you at supper."

I was glad _they_ knew what I meant about "personal nature," because _I_ sure didn't. The phrase had just jumped into my head. But I was happy it had worked. I didn't have much of an idea what was in the box, which was nailed securely shut, but for some reason or other I knew I didn't want either of them around — or anyone else, for that matter —

when I opened it. It was nothing personal; I just wanted to be the first to see what it contained.

As soon as I got it up to my room, I had to go back down and get a hammer out of Mrs. Dean's tool shed. Then I went to work. It was so heavily nailed up that it took me a good 15 or 20 minutes to get it open. Once I did, I found a chest with a locked lid, and taped on top, an envelope that held a key and a note that read:

Bobby,

This belonged to my grandfather, who died of scarlet fever in 1873. He left instructions that it was to go his great-great-grandson, your father's son. You. I cannot explain how he knew your father would have a son, but the old man was what we used to call "pixie-touched." The family knew that he practiced black magic, and it was a source of great disgust, and I suppose a little fear, for the rest of us.

The chest has been in the attic and unopened for many years. I know I do not have many more days on this earth, so I have gotten it down and followed his instructions before it becomes too late. Although the chest had not been opened for many decades, I peeked inside long enough to see that it contains some of his books. I hope they are something you can use.

Grandmother Frank

John, when I turned the key in that

ancient lock and opened up the chest, I was shocked. It was full of books, all right, along with pamphlets on old, browning parchment, sewn together. The smell that wafted up from that crumbling paper was indescribable — musty, strange, and ancient. It seemed to trigger a little of the seventh sense in me.

Carefully, I started exploring the stuff on top. It all seemed to be written in High German, which, with some effort, I can read well enough — as you might remember. I opened one of the books to the title page and saw that it dated clear back to the early 1700s, making it more than 200 years old. The pamphlets seemed to carry even more antiquity; as hard as it is to believe, I wouldn't be surprised if some of them went all the way back to the Middle Ages. These were very fragile, of course, and I handled them with as much gentleness as I could muster.

After a couple of hours of painstaking translation and careful study, I realized that there was only one thing that several of the ancient booklets could be. They were undoubtedly _grimoires_. That is, collections of incantations for long-ago magic spells.

It wasn't any time at all before I'd run onto a spell for — well, I guess the best translation would be "privacy." It called for me to start by drawing a simple pentagram on the floor. Digging around in my chest of drawers, I found the chalk I'd brought with me from Arkansas; and, just as in Mackaville,

I had a nice big throw rug beside my bed that would cover the star up just fine.

Unlike in Mackaville, though, I had a door to my room that I couldn't lock because of the fire-escape rules in D.C. I'd gotten used to not even worrying about that unlocked door; this time, though, just as I was finishing up the pentagram, I was surprised by a knock, followed by a "Hey, Robert." Then the door cracked open and Buster peered in, his eyes going to the chalk outline on the floor.

He'd caught me in the act, and there really wasn't anything for me to do but brazen it out. I guess I'd planned to tell Buster something about my "powers" at some point, but now my hand had been forced.

"C'm'on in, Buster," I said, as casually as I could. "Have a seat."

He looked a bit unsure as he hauled his bulk through the door, shutting it quietly behind him, and then sitting down on the edge of my bed. His eyes went from the pentagram to me to the box that sat atop my desk, and the books and pamphlets beside it. I could smell them; I'll bet he could, too.

"Know what this is?" I asked, nodding at the pentagram.

"A star?"

"Well, yeah. But more than that. Remember your <u>Weird Tales</u>."

He thought a minute, then nodded. "Oh, sure. Five points. That's a <u>pentagram</u>."

"Right."

"It's for magic."

"Right again."

He swallowed as his gaze met mine. "Okay. What are <u>you</u> doing with it?"

I may not have known Buster very long, but from our first meeting I've had the idea I could trust him. Maybe that's the seventh sense, maybe not, but I felt sure I was right. So, straightening up, I covered the pentagram with the rug, put the piece of chalk back in the drawer, shut it, and turned to face him.

"Clyde with you?" I asked.

"Naw. He's downstairs listening to <u>Blondie</u> with Mrs. Dean. I don't really care much for those comedies, so I thought I'd come up and see what you got from Railway Express. Don't mean to be nosy or nothin.' Don't want to interrupt anything, you know, of a <u>personal</u> nature," he said, using the same words I'd used on him and Clyde downstairs.

Clearly uneasy, he kept sneaking glances at the books and pamphlets on my desk. I let him look for a few seconds, and then, smiling, I said, "Well, honestly, this <u>is</u> kind of personal. What would you say if I told you I had — I guess you could call 'em special <u>abilities</u>? Things I can do that most people can't."

He grinned back in spite of himself. "Like the Shadow?" He asked. "Can you cloud men's minds?"

"Not exactly. But I know a little something about magic. In fact, I've been known to use it." I swept my hand toward the chest and its contents. "That's what these books are about."

His curiosity got the best of him, and he went over to the desk and touched the chest, tentatively. Eyeing the books and pamphlets, he started to reach toward them. But he drew back his hand.

"They look awfully old," he said.

"They are," I returned. "And they have some ancient spells in them. I was just getting ready to try one out — what amounts to a 'privacy' spell. You want to stick around and see if it works?"

His answer came quickly. "No. I don't think so. I just wanted to see what was in the chest."

"Okay," I told him. "Now you know — and you also know more about me than just about anyone else. I know I can trust you, but I'd sure appreciate it if you didn't share any of what I've just told you, even with our fellow boarders. They might not understand."

"You can trust me, Robert. Bank on it." He stuck out his mitt and I shook it.

"Thanks, Buster," I said, and then, "Sure you don't want to see what happens when I try out the spell?"

"I admit I'm a little <u>curious</u>, and maybe one of these days, if you ask me again, I'll take you up on an invitation like that," he returned. "But to be honest with you, I don't think I should right now. It's just a feeling, but I got to tell you it's an uncomfortable one. It's just that . . ."

He let his words trickle away, and I jumped in. "Believe me, I know how powerful feelings are, and how it's a good idea to listen to 'em.So I understand. Again, though, this is our secret."

"Our secret." He nodded. "See you later, Robert. Sherlock Holmes ought to be on about now." And with that, he was gone, headed back downstairs to listen to the boarding-house radio.

I shut the lockless door and sat down at the desk, looking over the grimoire I'd picked for this evening. And then I remembered what the spell was all about. It was a <u>privacy</u> spell.

I laughed out loud. I hadn't even started it yet, but if Buster's exit was any indication, it was already working.

And now, back to examining my preternatural gifts from a guy whose name I don't even know. I'll write more later, but probably not tonight. I'm too jazzed about what came out of that little chest and what it all could mean — and do.

Your friend and temporarily speechless correspondent,

Robert

October 18, 1939
Tuesday night

Dear John,

    Just when I thought things couldn't get
any weirder — well, they did. Ever since I
got that chest full of no-kidding real magic
stuff from Grandmother Frank, things have
come at me in waves. I don't yet know how
they're connected, or even if they have
anything in common at all, other than they're
happening to <u>me</u>.

    Let me go back to last night, after I
wrote you. I stayed up a little longer,
studying one of the faded pamphlets from the
stack of occult material until all the translating started giving me a headache. But
before I hit the hay, I recited the incantation for the privacy spell, the one I wrote
you about yesterday. I also said the words,
as well as I could pronounce 'em, for one
that offers what translates as "personal
protection." I muttered them both over the
chalked pentagram, and although I can't tell
you why or how, I knew immediately that they
were real and were going to work.

    It's clear to me that I've just scratched
the surface of what these books and pamphlets
contain, and I'm going to be doing a lot more
translating and investigating — and spell-

casting — over the next few weeks. What I've got here is nothing less than a treasure trove of pure magic. What a gift, and from someone I never met. In fact, I don't even know his name. I'll ask Pop in my next letter home.

I do remember something my old man told me about, though. There's a tradition in the Brown family of our men giving things to their unborn descendants. Like Grandmother Frank, I have no idea how this forbear of mine knew my dad would have a son. If he'd had a daughter instead, what would've happened to the writings? And now that I think about it, how would my great-great-grandfather have known that I'd be a willing recipient of ancient magic texts, which others might've just thrown away or given to a museum or something? It's a baffler, but I'm sure glad the old boy did what he did.

Today, pushing papers for the government seemed even more tedious than usual. The second hand of the big Seth Thomas wall clock across the room seemed to drag like an anchor, and it felt like days before I finally checked out. I didn't wait a second past 5 o'clock. I wanted to get back as soon as I could, eat a little supper, and get up to my room to go over more of the fantastic gifts from my ancestor.

As I was leaving the office, I caught old Fletch giving me the fisheye. I'm sure he's wondering why I'm not staying late and "turning to" like the eager beaver I used to be. I'm sure I'll start putting in some extra hours again, but right now just about all I can think of are the books and pamphlets concealed in the chest in the bottom drawer of my dresser. For good measure, I've cast a privacy spell over the chest itself. That means that if someone happens to start digging around in my chest of drawers, all that he'll find in the drawer will be underwear.

At least, that's the way I understand it.

You know, I didn't even care that we had meat loaf tonight. It seems to be the house specialty, and to give credit to Mrs. Dean, it always tastes a little different each time. She never fails to put out plenty of gravy, along with mashed potatoes, and she appears to favor canned creamed corn for our vegetable. We get that just about as much as we get her meat loaf.

Anyway, it was all I could do to keep from bolting my food and running up the stairs. But I managed to keep myself under control. It took some effort.

All the boarders were at the table tonight, and it was Nick, the book-of-the-month-loving older guy, who seemed to first notice my new time of arrival.

"You've sure gotten in early the past couple of days," he said, plopping a big dollop of mashed potatoes from the communal bowl onto his plate. "Is it that you can't get enough of our scintillating company?"

"Sure," I said with a grin. "Either that or the meat loaf."

"Or the creamed corn," added Clyde, raising a spoonful. That got a laugh. Luckily for us, Mrs. Dean was back in the kitchen, out of earshot. The last thing any of us wanted to do was hurt her feelings.

I glanced over at Buster, who busied himself with procuring another slice of the oatmeal-loaded entree. Of course, he was the only one in the boarding house who had an idea of why I was returning earlier these days, and the knowledge seemed to be weighing a bit heavily on him. We haven't said much to one another since he walked in on me and the pentagram yesterday evening; he hasn't been back up to see me since I told him about the magic books and my belief in them.

I guess I can't blame him. It's a lot to digest. More, even, than Mrs. Dean's meat loaf.

"I'm not trying to be nosy, understand," said Nick, who was being just that. "But for the past two days you've bolted your food and headed to your room, and we don't see you again. I know I speak for the rest of the fellows when I say we'd like to have you listen to the radio with us every once in a while or play some cards or something."

"Well, Nick," I returned, "I'll be honest

with you." Out of the corner of my eye, I saw Buster give a little start.

"You're an appreciator of literature, I know.So I'll let you know something I don't really want the world to know right now. I'm writing a book."

Buster grinned then, in spite of himself.

"A commendable undertaking," Nick said. "Will this be a serious novel, or one of the pulpwood-type adventure stories you and Buster seem to enjoy so much?"

"Can't tell you yet. But _I'm_ serious about it."

He nodded. "Good. Good. I wish you luck with it."

"Thank you. I know a lot of people announce that they're writers before they actually get anything down on paper, and I don't want you to think I'm one of those pretenders.So I just haven't said anything about it to anybody." I made a show of looking at my strap watch. "I'd better get started," I said. "I'm writing it longhand, so there won't be any typing to disturb anyone. Not yet, anyway."

I got up then and headed up the stairs, hoping my white lie would satisfy any curiosity Nick — and Clyde, for that matter — might have. I was banking on the idea that they knew you didn't disturb a writer while he was working.

I've thought about putting something in front of the door from inside my room, maybe my desk, just to slow down anyone that might be coming in. But I know that's against fire-department regulations, and if the person happened to be Mrs. Dean, having the fire exit blocked might be enough reason to put me out on the street. I didn't want to risk that.

The spell I was looking at tonight, once I got away from the dinner table, was one that you might call "pest control." As nearly as I can tell, it's something to keep away flies and other insects and even vermin. But I'm going to have to wait to find out, because of something that happened only about a half-hour ago.

My desk lamp gives off a yellow light that doesn't quite reach into the corners of my room at night. As I worked on the High German words in that little pamphlet, I realized that I was straining my eyes, squinting at that rusted-looking ink, so I got up to turn on the overhead bulb. Mrs. Dean, bless her frugal soul, only puts 40-watt bulbs in the overhead fixtures, but I've replaced mine with a 75-watter.

As soon as I clicked it on, with no warn-ing, the seventh sense rippled through me. I turned to the window and saw a pair of eyes staring at me!

I know. I know. It couldn't be. From my room, it's a good 20 feet to the pavement, and the window is six feet west of the exit stairs. Still, there they were, two huge, dark, liquid eyes, peering out from under my window shade. And as I watched, they started _flicking_ — back and forth, up and down, almost mechanical, like a metronome. And John, I'm not exaggerating when I say that they radiated pure evil.

Automatically, I reached into the top drawer of my bureau, dug with one hand under the socks and underwear, and grabbed up my Colt pistol.

I made the window in three strides. The bulging eyes, still searching my room, didn't appear to see me at all, and I understood suddenly that the privacy spell must be working! Throwing up the sash with an involuntary shout — as though I were trying to scare whatever it was away — I saw those hideous orbs flash up and lock into my own eyes. And then, like that, they were gone.

I peered down and caught a fleeting glimpse of something that looked like a giant ape or monkey, flashing around the corner of the boarding house; the porch blocked my view after that. I can tell you this, though: It wasn't human. It was big, maybe as tall as me — or even a little taller.

As I say, it's been nearly a half-hour now, and the tingling that runs from my scalp to my feet is just now subsiding, like a clock alarm finally running down. There's still a pounding in my chest, and I can't shake the notion that the creature is not of this earth, and that it will be back.

This felt _exactly_ like the reactions I had to the worst of the snakes and swine back in Arkansas. It's all I can do to keep myself from feeling small and helpless.So I've been trying to keep my mind focused on the privacy spell, and how it must've worked on whatever it was that tried to spy on me. I think it only saw me after I yelled; before that, it didn't seem to spot me at all, even though all the lights in the room were on. This is something I'm going to have to test to make sure; the instructions in the pamphlet indicated that the spell only worked on those who were _lautios_, which translates to "silent" or "noiseless." So it would make sense that the spell would be in effect until I uttered something.

There's a way to test this, and I'll probably do just that tomorrow night. I hate to use poor Buster as a guinea pig, but since he's the only one around who knows anything about magic and me, I don't have a lot of choices.

Of course, if _you_ were on the premises, we could get it done in a couple of New York minutes.

For that and many other reasons, wish you were here, chum.

But you're not, so I'm having a dialogue with myself, wondering, among other things, whether this . . . _visitation_ has anything to do with the magic books and the spells I've just started using? John, I don't know. I do know that I'm done with magic for the rest of tonight — except for reciting the words to that privacy spell again, just to make sure. And I'll not only be sleeping light tonight but also with a gun under my pillow, loaded with bullets of silver.

Your pal and faithful comrade,
Robert

October 20, 1939
Thursday night

Dear John,

I'm really beat, for reasons that will
shortly become evident. So if I sound a
little bit hurried in this missive, please
forgive me. There's lots to tell, and I don't
know if I'll be able to tell it to you before
I succumb to the arms of Morpheus. But I'll
do as much as I can.

As you might imagine, I didn't get a whole
lot of rest on Tuesday night. The thought of
those giant otherworldly eyes flashing around
my room, kept returning to my mind, making
sleep elusive. At one point, however, I had a
kind of brainstorm; I acted on it yesterday
afternoon after work, visiting a drugstore
near the federal building and putting down
fifteen cents for a large-sized jar of
Vaseline.

When I got home, I went right upstairs to
my room, opened the window, and smeared about
a half-inch of that petroleum jelly on the
three-inches-wide ledge of my west window,
where I'd seen those orbs peering in at me the
night before. Then, for good measure, I opened
up my north window and gave it the same treatment. Since there were no tall trees around,
my thought was that the ape-creature or what-

ever it was had to leap from either the ground or the porch to grab hold of the window ledge. I hoped it would be slick enough to cause the thing to tumble down and maybe incapacitate it long enough for me to run downstairs and get a good look at it.

After I'd done that, I thought of something else. I told you earlier that I'd found a protection spell in one of those ages-old pamphlets, and, without going into details, it seemed to be uncomplicated enough to try. So I once again uncovered the pentagram and recited the incantations for protection.

As I mentioned in my last letter, it seems to me that the privacy spell is negated once you speak, and then you have to renew it. It may be that it only stops if you speak in front of someone, as I did with the ape creature and Buster. If that was the case, I didn't figure it would do me much good to recite it and then go down to supper, where I'd be chatting with the other boarders.

I was hoping the same thing wasn't true for the protection spell. Before I cast it, I didn't see any references to <u>lautios</u> or <u>stumm</u> or any of the other German words that have to do with staying mute, so I took a chance, said the words, and kicked the rug back over the chalked pentagram on my floor.

That was the first thing I did at the boarding house that evening. The second was to take Buster aside before we all went in to

supper and ask him to come upstairs afterwards and not tell anyone.

Looking in at the table, where Clyde and
Nick were already seated, he whispered, "Is
this about . . . you know?"

"Yeah," I said. "Mum's the word, okay?"

He nodded, and we joined our fellow
boarders for a repast of what Mrs. Dean
announced as Salisbury steak, which bore an
uncanny resemblance to meat loaf shaped into
patties and covered with brown gravy. It
wasn't all that bad, truth to tell, and I
finished up and left for my room just as
Buster was refilling his plate.

Once I got inside, I uncovered the pentagram again and said the words for the privacy
spell. Then I turned on the overhead light,
got a back-issue <u>Dime Detective</u> out of my
desk drawer, and sat down in my chair to
wait, glancing more than I wanted to at my
west window and the gathering darkness
outside.

Buster must've really wolfed down his
second helping. I hadn't gotten through three
pages of the Marquis of Broadway story when I
heard a light tapping at my door. I didn't
say anything, and in a moment, Buster had
slowly cracked it open and was peering around
my room.

"Hey, Robert," he said, almost in a whisper. "You here?"

It was funny. He was looking right at me,

but he was looking <u>through</u> me. As far as he was concerned, I was nowhere around.

Stepping tentatively across the threshold, he pushed the door shut behind him and called my name again.

"Right here, Buster," I said.

He actually gasped. "Robert!" he said. "How'd you do that?"

I smiled. "Do what?"

"All of a sudden, it was just like you . . . <u>appeared</u> in that chair. I know it was empty just a second ago."

I gave him a smile I hoped was disarming, accompanied by a little shrug.

"Remember what I told you Monday night? That I not only knew a little something about magic, but I had also been known to use it?"

"Sure. I remember."

"I just used it, Buster. On you."

Silence hung in the air as he stared at me. Then, thankfully, he grinned back.

"I just got goose pimples the size of baseballs," he said, looking down at the back of his hands and flexing his fingers. "Guess you're the genuine article, all right."

I nodded. "Yeah. I am. And you're the only one in this house — just about the only person in the whole city, for that matter — who knows. In fact, I trust you so much that I kind of used you for a guinea pig. I hope you don't mind."

I proceeded then to give him a short explanation about the privacy spell and how I wanted to find out if it was canceled the moment I said anything out loud.

"You just saw the result," I said. "When I want to renew the privacy spell, I'll have to do it all over again, and it'll only last as long as I'm quiet. You helped me find that out, and I thank you."

He grinned again. "You're welcome, I guess. Are you going to do another disappearing act tonight?"

"I think I will. You want to watch?"

It took him what seemed like a long time to decide. In the moments before he spoke, I realized just how much I was asking from him. I knew he was seeing a lot that he couldn't understand, but I banked on him having the character and backbone to be able not only to absorb what he saw, but to keep silent about it.

"Yeah," he said, interrupting my thoughts. "I think so."

"All right," I returned. "You might stand in front of the door, just in case the other guys or Mrs. Dean gets nosy." Then, with his big body blocking the hallway entrance, I once again pushed back the rug, exposing the pentagram, and got to work.

I'll say this for Buster. All of this may have unnerved him, but he didn't let it show. He just watched, silently, as I repeated the words of the incantation and, apparently, disappeared before his eyes. Only then did his composure break.

"<u>Son-of-a-bitch</u>!" he whispered. "I'll be a ring-tailed son-of-a-bitch."

I started to say something to reassure him, catching myself just in time. It was a good thing, too, because only a few seconds later I heard an ear-splitting shriek coming from the direction of my west window, where I had seen those huge bulging eyes peering in a couple of nights earlier. As I sprinted the few steps toward the glass, I glanced back at Buster, still standing with his back to the door. That scream had been loud enough to wake the dead, but Buster seemed to not have heard anything at all. He was still staring at the spot where I'd just stood.

Then, suddenly, I was face to face with a nightmare.

The encounter only lasted a few seconds, but it'll be seared into my mind forever: a hideous face surrounded by bristles that looked like radio antennae, those giant malevolent eyes peering in, a mouth full of fangs, open and snarling as it floundered on the window ledge, struggling to get a grip with its clawlike, sharp-nailed hands.

And then, like that, it was gone. And a loud thump on the pavement told me that the Vaseline had worked. I jerked up the window and looked down in time to see more of the creature than I had the other night. It was maybe five feet seven, five feet eight, covered with wiry, dirty hair that looked orange in the glow of the streetlight. It was stooped, moving quickly away by using its hands and arms to flip itself forward, its big head, far out of proportion to its body, jiggling every time the thing advanced.

Surely, Buster had seen what I'd seen, but when I turned, his back was still against the door, although now he was looking toward the window — but not at _me_.

"What's going on, Robert?" he asked softly. "I saw the window go up. That must be you, huh?"

Of course, I couldn't say anything. I didn't want to break the privacy spell. Not until I was sure that creature wasn't returning.

"I'll be going now," he said, swallowing and taking one last look around the room. "I know you're here, and now I remember you can't talk because of the spell. So I'll see you later."

He slipped out then, and I knew he hadn't glimpsed the monkey creature; surely, he would've said something if he had. So there was another puzzler: Why could Buster not see the thing?

Clicking my room light off and sticking my head as far out of the window as I could, I scanned the area for any sign of the abomination that hadn't been able to get a handhold on my sill. As I looked, my eyes drifted to the little apartment over the garage where Mr. Saki, the house boy, lived. There was a light in his window.

Now, John, I had no intention of spying on that Japanese gentleman, but once I looked I couldn't turn away. As nearly as I could tell, he had a half-naked old woman, with long stringy hair, in the room with him. At first, I couldn't tell much about her; it was mostly the grey hair, which ran more than halfway down her back, and the brief glimpses of terribly saggy wrinkled bosoms that gave her away as a member of the opposite sex. She was turned away to the extent that I couldn't see her face, but I <u>could</u> make out what I can only describe as a skirt made out of sticks. That's right — sticks, tied at the waist with strips of what looked to be fur of some kind. And there seemed to be calabash gourds hanging around her waist, painted in all sorts of different colors, along with some little bags.

Over her weathered shoulder, I could see Mr. Saki, who seemed to be talking fervently with her, his face animated, his hands clenching and unclenching.

"Good Lord," I muttered to myself, realizing too late that I had shattered my privacy spell with those two quiet words.

And at that exact moment, she turned — and locked eyes with me!

John, I can't begin to tell you what I saw in those eyes. It was worse than the ape orbs that had peered in at me for two nights. I had never seen an uglier face. Even all the way across the back yard and the alley, I could see a mouth that stretched from ear to ear, filled with the black stumps of teeth, that seemed to be <u>snarling</u> at me. Her eyes bulged almost out of her head, and she let out a screech. I could barely hear it from my vantage point, but I knew it was meant for me.

And my seventh sense began clanging like a five-alarm-fire bell.

I saw Mr. Saki grab for her arm, just as I tried to pull down the shade, to cut off her awful gaze. But I never got that far. In a twinkling, she shook him off and pointed her index finger at me, just as you'd point a sword. An arc of intense white light sprang out and speared me in the chest, dead center. It whammed me with the force of a Mack truck barreling down a mountain. I dropped like a sack of cement, and then I died.

Okay, not really. But there was lots more to come, and I'll tell you all about it in my next letter.

Reliving that still-fresh scene has worn me out, and this old feather bed of Mrs. Dean's has never looked better. I promise I'll be back in good time, after I catch a lot more than forty winks.

Your pal and very nearly dispatched comrade.

Robert

October 21, 1939
Friday night

Dear John,

It's finally the weekend, and I've already turned down an offer from Buster to accompany him to the flying tintypes tonight. He's found a second-run movie house here in D.C. that shows those B-grade saddle operas you and I used to love to watch back in Hallock; turns out he's a fan as well. Just another reason to like the guy.

But, instead of taking in a Three Mesquiteers picture (with the promising title of _The Kansas Terrors_) and a Tim McCoy "Lightning Bill Carson" with my fellow tenant at _chez_ Dean, I'm writing to catch you up on the events in Robert's life over the past couple of days. I'd say that it's going to be hard for you to believe, but I guess I know better by now.

My apologies for leaving you last time with a cliffhanger worthy of a Republic serial. Like any good Republic hero, I wiggled out of it and lived to fight another day. Although, truth to tell, I wasn't sure at all of what the outcome would be.

After that blast of blinding white light from the finger of that ancient woman exploded inside my head, I went out, and the

next thing I knew was a knocking sound, soft
but insistent, almost in a cadence. It kept
up as I slowly came to, opening my eyes to
darkness.

Then, I almost panicked. Was I blind? Had
that flash taken away my sight?

Thankfully, even without my full powers of
reasoning, I remembered that little night
light in the electrical socket under my desk,
and with some effort I turned my head toward
it. What a relief it was to see its feeble
glow! I didn't know how long I'd been uncon-
scious, but I knew it was still nighttime.

At about that time, the knocking stopped.
Then, I watched as the door to my porch began
to slowly open.

Now John, I've told you that I have to
keep both my hall door and porch doors open
because of the fire regulations, but I have a
latch in my room that lets me lock the porch
door from the inside. In other words, people
always have to be able to open it from my
room and get out, but anyone on the outside
can't get in when it's locked — and I always
keep it locked, just on general principles.

Now, though, as I watched, it was opening.
I tried to push myself up off the cold floor
but just couldn't muster the strength. As the
door creaked, all I could think of was the
opening for _Inner Sanctum_. And I fervently
wished I'd hear the voice of that that
creepy announcer, making some sort of a pun
about death and horror, instead of my having

to face something that was actually happening.

As the door opened wide enough for me to glimpse the half-moon peeping through, a shape slipped into my room, which I recognized as Mr. Saki. The little Japanese leaned over me, his eyes open wide, and he exclaimed: "A, kare wa ikite imasu." (Yes, I looked up the spelling.) Roughly translated, that's pretty much the Colin Clive line from Frankenstein: "It's alive!" And there was about the same amount of amazed inflection in those Oriental words.

As he bent over me with a look of astonishment, I tried to say something, but all I could get out was a kind of gurgle. He blinked at me a couple of times and looked up and down my body before reaching beneath me and helping me get to my feet for the couple of steps it took me to get to the bed. I wavered when he let go of me but managed to stay upright.

"I do not understand, Robert," he said wonderingly. "You should be dead."

I shook my head slowly. "I'm not dead," I replied. "But I'm sure hurting some."

"I should not wonder. The Yamamba shot enough lightning at you to kill ten men. I cannot understand why you are not with your ancestors — but I am most relieved, my young friend."

Managing a weak smile, I said, "Not half as relieved as I am. Thanks, though."

Besides feeling like I'd been hit repeatedly by a sack full of bricks, I was getting all my senses back, and my mind was starting to fire on all its cylinders again. I squeezed my eyelids together for a long time, trying to clear my head, and when I opened them, the light was on in the room and Mr. Saki had pulled up my desk chair and was holding out a glass of water he must've gotten from the hall bathroom. I swallowed the liquid gratefully; found that it helped me to speak more clearly.

"What hit me, Mr. Saki?" I asked him. "What was it that old witch threw at me?"

"She is no witch, Robert," he returned. "The Yamamba is a spirit of the mountain — an earth spirit, if you will. Ordinarily, she is not evil. But she is dangerous, and she has what you might call a very short fuse, especially when it comes to those she does not know nor like. She did not know you when she saw you looking at her, and she reacted as she will. I tried very quickly to tell her about you, but she did not heed my words — until after. She was sure she had killed you, and she was remorseful, I think."

As I listened to him, the aches I'd been feeling all over seemed to coalesce into a tight fist somewhere around my solar plexus. I winced and, involuntarily, grabbed my chest. Waves of pain radiated from under my closed fist.

"We had better make sure she didn't blast

a hole in you, Robert," said Mr. Saki, gently. "Please unbutton your shirt."

When I'd done that, I looked down to see an angry red welt about the size of my hand, right there in the middle of my chest.

"Ah, yes." Mr. Saki said. He lowered his head and peered at the wound, then gently pressed it with an index finger. The sudden surge of pain was electric; I almost jumped out of my skin.

"I am sorry," he said. "But I see it is only superficial. Do you have ointment?"

"There's a tin of Unguentine in my top dresser drawer," I said.

While he was digging it out, I said, "Now, how about this — what? — Yamamba, you called her?"

He nodded and passed the tin to me.

"She's not a witch."

"No."

"She's a spirit?"

"Yes."

"What else can you tell me about her?" I asked, rubbing a good amount of Unguentine onto the welt, as lightly as I could. Immediately, the pain began ebbing.

"Much," he said, taking the tin and replacing it in my drawer. "Would you rather hear it another time, when you're better?"

"I'm fine now," I returned. "Shoot."

He nodded. "Very well. But I do not think you will believe it."

"Try me."

"It begins when I am ten years old or so," he said. "One day, I go up into the mountain near our home to explore and play, taking along hirugohan — I am sorry, a lunch — of rice, fish, and tofu that Mother had packed for me. I had only been up in the mountains for a few minutes when, suddenly, from behind a Sugi tree, the Yamamba stepped out, looking just as you see her now.

"Of course, I had heard the stories of the mountain spirit. All the children in my village had. And one of the things we'd heard is that if she was hungry when you met her, she would eat you. So I was very scared. I did not want to be eaten."

"I can understand that," I said, and the ghost of a smile flickered briefly across his face.

"Yes. So what was I to do? Very quickly, I unwrapped my meal and held it out to her, hoping that she might take it instead of eating me. I remember how my hand and arm were shaking as I watched her look at me and then at the food I was offering. Suddenly, she snatched it away and shoveled it down her throat, rice dripping down her chin. And she looked so comical that I suddenly laughed. Her head went up, her eyes bored into mine, and then — she laughed, too!"

He smiled again, a longer one this time. "From that day forward, we were friends. I didn't know it at the time, but she saw my offering of food — even though I thought I was doing it simply to save my own skin — as a gesture of kindness, and it sealed a bond of friendship between us that has lasted to this day. She was hungry, and I fed her. She has never forgotten. Many times in one year she still visits me."

"Well?" He raised his eyebrows. "Do you believe any part of my story?"

"Mr. Saki, honestly, I believe it <u>all</u>," I told him.

"Thank you. Just as your country's folk-lore, or mythology, is grounded in truth, so is ours. You have what have often been called elementals. Earth spirits. My Yamamba is one of those, and as a spirit of the mountain she commands all kinds of natural forces. Lightning is just one of them."

"Where is she now?"

"In my room. She is . . . contrite, after finding out that you were my friend. She is sure that she killed you." His eyes narrowed. "I was sure as well. Please pardon my boldness, but how is it you are still alive?"

At that point, John, my mind began racing. Should I tell him the truth — or, at least, the truth as I saw it? I was only seared when I should've been fried, and I was convinced it was the protection spell that had done the trick. But if I told him about the spell, I would have to tell him that I was, well, <u>different</u> — a magic man, a warlock, whatever he'd want to call me.

Then I remembered he'd just spent several

minutes talking about a mythological creature that was not only actually in the land of the living but was also his friend. And that's when I decided the hell with it.

"Mr. Saki," I began, "I have some, well, some magical and supernormal powers. I just recently learned a spell for personal protection, and it was in effect when your Yamamba sent that bolt of lightning into me." I started to say something about the books and pamphlets I'd been studying, which were now safe in my bottom dresser drawer, and thought briefly about kicking back my rug and showing him the pentagram I'd chalked on the floor. But I held back. After all, he didn't need to know <u>everything</u>.

"So now," I concluded, I'm asking <u>you</u> to believe <u>me</u>."

He nodded. "Ahhh, yes, that must be it. Magic against magic. That is a fine explanation." Then, "How do you feel now?"

Flexing my fingers and stretching my arms, I found that the pain was almost gone. Even the middle of my chest, where the Unguentine was doing its stuff, felt better.

"I think I'll live," I said. "Thank you for your help."

"It would be prudent for you to continue under that protection spell," he said, rising to go. "It could save your life again. I will explain it to Yamamba; she will be very intrigued. I suspect she will want to meet you."

The image of that hideous face and the pendulous wrinkled breasts nearly sent a chill through me, but I managed to sound sincere enough when I told him, "It would be a pleasure, Mr. Saki."

"And now, please to get some sleep. We both have work tomorrow."

"We do. And thanks again."

He had already turned toward the outside door when I thought of something. "Mr. Saki," I said. "Do you know anything about any ape-looking creatures? They wouldn't be traveling with your mountain spirit, would they?"

Turning to me, his face bland, he asked, "__Ape__-looking?"

"Yes." I gave him a quick description.

"They are not with Yamamba."

"I just started seeing them yesterday. They've been peering in my window. Is it only coincidence that they started haunting this boarding house at the same time your lady friend appeared?"

He fell silent for a moment. And when he spoke, it seemed to me he was choosing his words very carefully.

"When did you first begin casting your magic spells?"

"Only a couple of days ago," I said, once again almost mentioning the books before I stopped myself.

"Ah. Perhaps it is that. Your magic. You see, they have been around this city for a time. Please do not ask me how I know. I think they came here, to your window, because they felt the presence of some new . . . <u>supernaturalism</u> in the air and tracked it to you. However, I cannot be sure."

"What I can be sure of is this," he added, his eyes narrowing. "They are not apes. They are demons. You should avoid all contact with them. And that is all I can tell you."

Of course I had other questions, but before I could ask them, just like that he was gone. I still had a few hours before work, but I didn't know if I could relax enough to get any sleep. My mind was besieged with images — the Yamamba, the monkeys, Mr. Saki, the sizzling bolt from his window. Gingerly, with all these things rolling through my brain, I arose from the bed, went to the stairway door, and reached for the latch.

It was still locked.

More tomorrow from your pal and bemused correspondent,

Robert

October 22, 1939
Saturday morning

Dear John:

Turned in right after I wrote you last night, and, finally, got in a nice stretch of sleep. Yesterday there was a cold snap; we haven't even gotten to Hallowe'en yet here in the Nation's Capital and it already feels like winter's breathing down our necks. Good old Mrs. Dean brought me a couple of extra quilts yesterday afternoon, and I sure enjoyed having them. Burrowing in under a stack of covers reminded me of those frigid Minnesota nights and sleeping like only a kid can sleep.

I explained in my last missive why I wasn't able to get much rest Wednesday night, what with the Yamamba trying to knock me off the face of the earth and, before that, those monkey creatures peering through my window panes. After Mr. Saki left that night, I was a little unnerved, to say the least, and between looking toward the window every hour or so and hurting from the shot I'd taken from the ugly old witch — pardon me, <u>spirit</u> — a few hours of uninterrupted sleep just weren't in the cards.

But then came Thursday. I was going to write you about everything that happened then in my last letter, but there was so much to tell about Wednesday night that I was pooped by the time I got all of that down on paper. Luckily, Friday — yesterday — was uneventful, so this letter should catch you up on the Washington D.C. adventures of Robert the Rogue.

I was, as you imagine, pretty draggy on Thursday, thanks to the loss of sleep and, well, the _other_ factors I wrote you about. I admit to doing a lot of clock-watching and drinking a couple more Cokes than usual for lunch, just hoping for a little added pep. But then, funny enough, a little bit before five p.m. I dove into a stack of requisitions for Fort Sill, Oklahoma, and got it in my head that I was going to have every one of them typed up before I left. I was just about to finish the task when I became aware of old Fletch with his Moe Howard haircut bending over my desk.

"Well, Robert," he said, "I'd started to get a little worried about your commitment to your job. Looks like my worry was misplaced."

I glanced up at the clock and saw it was well past 6 p.m. You know how I can start concentrating on something, even reading a book, and lose all track of time and every-thing that's going on around me. That's what had happened when I dove into those requisi-tions. Looking around, I saw that the office was deserted except for the boss and me. Then I realized he was actually _smiling_.

"I just thought I'd finish up this batch of requisitions before I called it a day, Mr. Fletcher. So I can start fresh tomorrow, you know." I sounded like one of those <u>Our Gang</u> kids, trying to apple-polish the new teacher.

"Very commendable," he said. "But we're going to have to close up now. It's my son's birthday, and the missus and I are having a little party for him this evening. His friends from school are probably already there."

It was a little funny to think of old Fletch having a family, but I was kind of glad he did. I grinned back at him. "Sure, Mr. Fletcher," I said. "Tell him 'happy birthday' for me."

He almost beamed. "Certainly, Robert. Thank you."

We walked out the door together, and then he went to get his car, and I began what would be a twenty-minute wait for a street car. As I said, we've had a cold snap, and I was more than ready to get in when it finally pulled up. It was an older model than the one I usually caught but clean and warm anyway, with a lot fewer riders than I was used to at the end of the usual work day.

The ride home took about 25 minutes, and by the time I got there, supper was over and no one was around but Nick, who was sitting in front of the radio in the living room, improving his mind by listening to the <u>Ask It Basket</u> quiz show. He gave me a wave and asked me to join him, but I told him no thanks, that I was fagged and hitting the hay early.

About that time, Mrs. Dean popped her head out of the kitchen and motioned to me. I went in and saw that she'd put together another of her meat loaf sandwiches for me.

"Thought you might need this," she said. "I'll get you a glass of milk. Help you sleep."

"That's nice of you, Mrs. Dean. Thanks."

"Work late?"

"Yes, ma'am."

She nodded, handing me the glass. Thanking her, I picked up the plate and headed up the stairs, planning on a nice quiet meal and maybe a few pages of pulpwood adventure before drifting off to dreamland under Mrs. Dean's raggedy but comforting old quilts.

It was, however, not to be. As I went up the stairs and headed for my room, Mr. Saki suddenly appeared in front of me, out of the shadows. Even though he was smiling, it was a bit unnerving. I sloshed a little of the milk on the carpet, and he quickly produced a handkerchief, bent down, and wiped it up, saying, "My apologies, Robert. I should have spoken earlier so you knew I was here."

"It's fine, Mr. Saki."

He straightened, tucking the handkerchief back into his pants pocket. "You will have a visitor tonight," he said, the smile never leaving his face.

"Oh?"

"Yes. She wants to make sure you hold no grudge before she visits."

Instinctively, my hand went to my chest, where the bolt had struck the night before. His eyes widened a little.

"Naw," I said. "No grudge."

He nodded. "She is very mysterious, this Yamamba, and I say this as her friend of long standing. She asks that I do not accompany her on her visit. She prefers to . . . encounter you alone."

"All right," I told him. "But I have to ask you, Mr. Saki. Am I safe with her? She's not going to get mad and try to fry me again, is she?"

"I believe not. As I told you yesterday, she is contrite. Also, she knows you have magic."

"So why does she want to be alone with me?"

He shrugged and shook his head, still smiling. "I do not know. Perhaps you will ask her. Goodnight, my young friend." And like that, he was gone.

Well, I went on to my room, turning over what he'd told me in my mind, and I'd no sooner set the plate and glass down on my desk when there was a soft but unmistakable knock at the door.

You'll understand my surprise when I tell you that when I opened it an attractive, middle-aged Japanese woman in a blue silk kimono stood in front of me — the Yamamba, I knew, in a different (and far more appealing) guise. But she didn't stand for long. I'd no more opened up when she briskly pushed past me into my room, looking around with a gaze I can only describe as intense. It was like she was trying to take everything in at once. Then, she turned and faced me with the same direct stare. After a few moments of scrutinizing me, she stepped right up and poked me in the chest, exactly where her bolt had hit me the night before. It was still tender, and I flinched a little bit, which caused her to rattle off some Japanese.

I shook my head, trying to indicate that I couldn't speak the language. She tried again. I shook my head again. Her eyes narrowed and I thought I caught a flash of anger — the last thing I wanted. My seventh sense wasn't kicking in, which was good, but I didn't know what I could do to break the impasse.

Then, it hit me. She was standing on the rug, and I gestured to her to move off of it. When she got the idea and stepped away, I pulled it back and revealed the pentagram on the floor. She seemed to understand at once, quickly kneeling down and tracing over it with her finger, all the while making exclamations in the language of her country. Standing back up, she nodded, and then, giving me that narrowed-eye look again, she walked to the outside door, opened it, and emitted a sound that I can only describe as part-whistle, part-birdcall, a kind of weird trilling — like the sound Doc Savage makes, maybe, when he's concentrating hard on something. Then she stood listening, the cold wind whipping up around her and into my room. It was starting to get pretty frigid in there when, suddenly, a mongrel dog leapt into the room and stood, looking from the Yamamba to me.

She shut the door then, and I looked at the hound. I was pretty sure I'd seen him around the neighborhood. Given the fact he had no collar and his rib bones were showing through his brownish fur, I knew he was a stray, abandoned by his owner and forced to fend for himself in the city. There's got to be an especially warm spot in hell for people who walk away from their pets.

You know I'm a sucker for dogs, John — just like you. And there was something in his eyes that drew me in. I suddenly recalled being back in Arkansas and being able to communicate with the dogs that surrounded me when I visited the Destruiodras. Somehow, I knew that I could do the same thing with this mutt, if he was receptive.

That's when I remembered the meat loaf sandwich and glass of milk on my desk. I'd read somewhere that milk could cause dogs stomach discomfort, so I left the glass but set the plate with the big sandwich down in front of him. In maybe three bites, he'd gobbled it up. _Inhaled_ might be a better term.

I looked up to see the Yamamba — in her disguise as a regular woman, remember — nodding and smiling approvingly at me. And then, as clear as the ringing of a bell, the dog saying, "Thank you, sir." Or, rather, <u>thinking</u> it.

And then: "I'm here to help the two of you talk." I looked at the Yamamba, and she nodded, a big smile creasing her face. "She knows one way of speaking, you another," the mutt continued. "I can understand you both."

Yeah, John, I know how this sounds. But the long and short of it was that the Yamamba had invited the dog up to be nothing less than an <u>interpreter</u>. I know it would've been much easier for her to have used Mr. Saki, her friend, but for whatever reason she wanted to see me by herself. So the dog, sated by Mrs. Dean's sandwich, settled himself down on the floor, head raised, and became our conduit; for the next half-hour or so, we actually talked, without saying a word, through him. I decided to tell her about the ancient protection spell I'd gotten from my great-great grandfather — I even opened the drawer and showed the books and pamphlets to her — and she said, basically (through the dog), that I must be a young warlock.

The thought I gave back to her was, "Yes, but I'm pretty much a beginner."

She smiled. "Would you open your shirt?"

When I did, she softly touched the scar

and then said, or thought, "The bolt I sent through you should have killed you. But it only burned you a little. That spell you have is most effective. I am glad Saki has a friend so well-versed in magic. But why were you spying on us?"

Suddenly, the image of that old, horribly ugly, half-naked crone I'd seen through Mr. Saki's window came back to me. It was hard to reconcile that vision with the middle-aged woman now seated on the chair at my desk, while I sat on the bed facing her, the dog between us on the floor. Somehow, she sensed what I was thinking and sent this thought: "I have two appearances. This is one of them. The other is my real self. This one."

Like lightning, the woman sitting across from me became the Yamamba I'd seen through Mr. Saki's window — the one that had sent the electric bolt through my window, and almost through _me_. Up close, John, she was even _more_ hideous, and I couldn't help but jump at the sight of her. A deep, earthy smell accompanied the transformation, filling my nostrils. She grinned a black, toothless grin, fingering the sticks that formed the covering below her naked pot belly. I tried not to look at her body, those pendulous wrinkled breasts, but her face wasn't much of an improvement.

"I am more comfortable this way," she said through the dog, and I fought the urge to squeeze my eyes shut.

Swallowing, I managed to say — again, _think_ — "That's fine. You're my guest, and you should be comfortable."

"But you did not answer me, Robert Brown. Why were you spying on us?"

Quickly, I outlined my innocence, explaining how I was looking for any sign of the ape creature that had peered into my window that night. As she listened, she began nodding her wizened head.

"You are innocent then of any bad intentions. We shall be friends. There is much on the horizon in this city, and across the world. Will you help me keep Saki safe?"

I nodded. "I have deep regard for Mr. Saki and will be glad to do that." Then, the thought hit me. "Would you tell me something of that monster that peered at me through the window?"

She frowned then, and a growl issued from her throat, which, truth to tell, spooked me a little. The room smelled like we were in a cave, loamy mud piled all around us.

"I will tell you those are demons. Killers. They exist only to murder and destroy; avoid any contact with them. They were attracted to you because they sensed your magic."

I recalled that Mr. Saki had said that to me the night before, only in different words.

"Perhaps," she continued, "they have seen you and now their curiosity is satisfied. If that is so, do nothing to attract their attention. If it is at all possible, leave them alone. That is all I can tell you."

And then, John, just like that, she was gone. I don't mean she got up and left. I mean she <u>disappeared</u>, leaving behind only a faint odor of that wet earthiness.

The dog looked up at me and — I'll swear — shook his head, as though he couldn't believe it either. I reached down and scratched him behind his ears, thinking of the old dog I had for so many years back in Hallock. Remember Butch, the cocker spaniel? Well, there's a new Butch now, and while there may be some cocker spaniel in him, he's Heinz 57 all the way.

"Well, Butch," I said to him — the first time I'd spoken out loud for several minutes — "I guess we'll be pals now, all right? You can call me Robert. I called you Butch. Is that okay with you?"

I saw a flicker of something in his big dog eyes. It was surprise, I think, quickly giving way to sadness. It rolled through me, and for a few moments I felt that sadness myself, coupled with an agonizing sense of loneliness. While it quickly dissipated, it was a powerful shot.

"How did you know?" The words came into my head as he looked unwaveringly at me.

"Know what?" I asked without speaking.

"My name <u>is</u> Butch. The people I lived with, Jay and Janie and their father, they called me Butch. Janie cried and cried when

they moved away and left me here. Jay tried
not to, but he did. I saw him, twisted around
in the back seat of the car, looking through
the big window as they drove off — looking at
me and waving and crying. I couldn't talk to
them like I can to you. All I could do was
wag my tail until they disappeared. But I
loved them. I hope they are okay."

"I'm sure they are," I thought back. "I'm
glad you're with _me_ now. And that I didn't
change your name."

In response, his tail began to thump
against my floor. "Me, too. I will always be
close by." Then he padded to the outside door
and stood, just like any other dog would,
until I let him out. As he scrabbled down the
back stairs, I stood there in the darkness,
listening to the sounds of the city,
reflecting on the two visitors I'd just had.

Maybe not just visitors. Maybe friends.
United by what? Magic, I guess. Or something
beyond that — something powerful and even
unnamable? Hell, I didn't even know if I'd
somehow divined Butch's real name, or if it
was just a coincidence. And that was the
least of the mysteries I'd just confronted.

So that was my Thursday. I'm going for a
little walk now out behind the boarding
house, where Butch has taken up residence
under the garage. Since we became pals, he's
been getting Ken-L Ration out of cans, and
believe me, he's a sucker for that horse
meat. I think he'll enjoy an early lunch.

I figure it's the least I can do for my interpreter. And my friend.

Your faithful correspondent and fellow dog lover,

Robert

October 23, 1939
Sunday afternoon

Dear John,

Strap yourself in, chum, because your old pal has had himself one hell of an adventure. I may not have been laughing in the face of danger like the Scarlet Pimpernel, but there was plenty of it — danger, I mean, and I guess a little laughter too, now that I think about it. I intend to tell you all about it, no matter how many pages it takes, so get comfortable. I might recommend a libation at your side — like Dan Turner, Hollywood Detective says, a jorum of skee — along with plenty of good light.

It started quietly enough. I think I told you earlier that Buster had wanted me to go to the movies to see a couple of oaters with him Friday night, and I passed. Well, as things turned out, Nick found him listening to the radio after dinner and _he_ asked Buster if he wanted to see a movie with _him_.

I've told you about Nick, the oldest one of us boarders, and his disdain for lowbrow literature like the pulps we love. I guess that goes for motion pictures as well, because when Buster brought up the idea of seeing the western-movie double bill, Nick quickly disabused him of that notion, saying that they must take in <u>The Rains Came</u>, a big A-picture based on a big novel that of course Nick had read.

Buster told me all about it Saturday, after we'd fixed ourselves some sandwiches Dagwood Bumstead would've been proud to build. When I first moved in, a couple of weeks ago, Mrs. Dean told me I'd be on my own for Saturday lunches, since that's the day she does all her shopping and she's not around. But I guess her conscience started bothering her or something, because earlier this week she told us all she was going to start leaving some sliced meat and cheese for us on Saturdays. She was as good as her word. When Buster and I opened up her refrigerator, we found pimento loaf, thick-sliced ham, salami, and two kinds of cheese waiting for us. Mmm-mmm good, as the Campbell Soup people like to say.

"I knew that Myrna Loy was the star of <u>The Rains Came</u>," Buster said as we settled down at the dining-room table with our sandwiches and a couple of big glasses of milk. It was after one o'clock, and I guess Nick and Clyde had eaten earlier. Anyway, they weren't around.

"Remember what a dish she was in <u>Mask of Fu Manchu</u>? — boy, she was an evil one, but beautiful. She went to the top of my hit parade after that."

"Fah Lo See," I returned with a grin.

"That was her name in the picture. Boris Karloff's daughter."

"Right you are. So I thought what the hell, and I said I'd go. It was at one of those big palaces — the Ambassador. Very hoity-toity. Cost me two bits to get in, and there wasn't even a second feature. Of course, with Nick it was Dutch treat."

"Worth a quarter?" I asked.

He thought for a moment. "Yeah. Well, I dunno. I guess. It was long and there was lots of drama and a big earthquake, a flood, and cholera. Plus, Myrna Loy's still a looker, and a girl named Brenda Joyce was worth a few gazes herself. So maybe I got my money's worth." He grinned. "But after all that classy stuff, I think I could use a couple of saddle operas to cleanse the palate, as they say. You game?"

Grinning back, I said, "Yeah. I'm game."

He looked at his strap watch. "It's Saturday, so they're running those two pictures I told you about, with cartoons and serial chapters and the whole nine yards. You want to go now? Or you want to wait until the curtain-climbers go home?"

"Now's as good a time as any," I said. "I wonder if those Saturday matinees are still full of spitballers, like they were back in Hallock."

"Or Milk Dud chuckers," Buster returned. "One way to find out, I guess."

Finishing up our lunch and carrying the

glasses and plates back to the sink to wash 'em off, we set sail for the picture show.

Even with my leather jacket and a light sweater, I was almost cold. Once we got inside the heated street car, though, I warmed up pretty fast. By the time the conductor let us off, right in front of the old theater that sat in the middle of a less fashionable block, I was plenty comfortable.

"Not quite as classy as your destination last night," I said, glancing up at the marquee. The wind was blowing pretty good, and it had knocked the second "G" off THE FIGHTING RENEGADE, so it read "RENE ADE," and some of the other letters in both titles sat crookedly, like tired old men, moving a little with every gust.

"Yeah," he returned, "but not quite as expensive, either." He nodded toward the ticket booth, on which a hand-written sign proclaimed, "KIDS UNDER 12 5 CENTS, ADULTS 10 CENTS."

"I'll have enough left out of a quarter to get some Milk Duds to throw," I said.

"And a big dill pickle," Buster said, laughing.

We were in high spirits. I felt like a kid again. And then, as we stepped up to the give our money to the old granny behind the window, I heard the sound of a fife and drum in the distance. Looking that way, I saw a group of maybe a dozen Bund members, all decked out in their black and white outfits and garrison caps with the red Nazi symbols. A couple of them were playing the instruments, with the rest marching along. Two more out in front carried stacks of what looked to be leaflets. While the others marched behind them, that pair worked either side of the street, forcing their propaganda sheets into the hands of anyone who'd stand still long enough. Since it was a Saturday afternoon, the sidewalks were fairly full, so there was no shortage of marks.

"Well, would you look at <u>that</u>," I said, stepping away from the booth and almost running into a couple of kids behind us. "C'm'on, Buster. Let's go get some of what those Nasties are passing out."

He looked up the street. "Bund," he said with a sneer. "Hell, I don't want anything to do with those crazy S.O.B.'s. Let's go in."

"No, no, you don't get it," I returned, holding out an arm to block him. "The more flyers we get, the fewer they have left to pass out. And once we get 'em, we can raise a ruckus about what they contain. Cause a stink. It might make life a little more difficult for those goose-stepping bastards — temporarily, at least."

Buster shrugged. "All right. I'm with you."

"Good. Let's go."

In retrospect, maybe we should've paid our money and disappeared into the theater instead. When I got a little closer to the guy working our side of the street, my seventh sense started rattling around inside me and I realized with a start that it was my old neighbor Elrich. You remember, John — I not only landed several lucky blows on his carcass in that fight outside Mr. Gold's store; I also swore out a complaint for his arrest. I guess they'd kept him in lockup for a while, but his heil-Hitler pals must've gotten the geetus together to spring him.

I made him out before he saw me, and Buster stepped up and said, "Hey, how about fixing me up with some copies of your literature? The guys back at the dorm need some new reading material."

Elrich's little pig eyes lit up at that — and then blazed when he looked over Buster's shoulder and saw me.

"You!" he said. Actually, he spit it more than he said it.

"Hello, neighbor," I returned, grabbing at a handful of brochures. "How's Adolph these days?"

Pulling the material out of my reach and clutching it to his chest, he shouted, "Swine! You damn no-good lousy son-of-a—"

"Easy," I interrupted. "There are young ears around."

Sure enough, a few lads, headed for the theater, had stopped to gaze up at us. I could see some adults wandering down the sidewalk toward us as well.

Elrich looked like he wanted to bite

nails. His puffy face was red and he was almost gasping. Meanwhile, the guy passing out the literature on the other side of the street had crossed to where we were, wondering, I'm sure, what the fuss was all about. Buster reached over and took a couple of brochures as the guy passed him.

If smoke could really come out of someone's ears, like it does in the Warner Brothers cartoons, Elrich would've been smoking like a three-alarm fire.

"What is this?" asked his Nazi pal, who'd begun to look alarmed.

"This — this — _verdammte_ mugg is the gink who gave us all the trouble outside that kike's store," Elrich said. "I spent a night in the cooler because of him. You remember the sixty smackers you had to raise to get me out? This is the dirty s.o.b. who's responsible."

Then, inexplicably, his face lit up with an evil smile.

"You got a price on your head, pally," he said to me. "A big C-note — but only if you're _dead_!"

My seventh sense seemed to be cooling a little, indicating that he probably wouldn't do anything but talk — at least for the present. So putting all the condescension in my voice that I could muster, I said, "Pleased to hear there's a reward out on me. But don't think for a minute that you or any of the rest of these costumed clowns'll collect it."

By this time, the remaining Bund members had arrived, and they grumbled threateningly at my characterization of their wardrobes. But there were also maybe a dozen other people around at that time, and I was banking on the idea that none of the little Nazis had the guts to take me on in front of all those witnesses. While Elrich stood there, stiff as a rod, I grabbed the sheaf of brochures he was holding and, with a flourish, dropped them in a trash basket that stood on the sidewalk just outside the theater.

At the same time, Buster, who'd been pretending to read a flyer, exclaimed, "Holy crap! This is all lies — <u>big</u> ones! If I brought this garbage into the dorm, they'd kick me out." Then, looking at the assembled Bund members, he said, "You all ought to be ashamed of yourselves." At the same time, he tore the handouts in two and threw them on top of the ones I'd just disposed of.

Then, he turned to the crowd and said, "Folks, these are <u>Nazis</u>!"

I guess it was the element of surprise, or maybe all the witnesses. Elrich hated my guts, of course, and maybe he could've rallied the troops against Buster and me, but he didn't. He just stood there, gnashing his teeth.

Then, behind me, came an older guy's voice: "Lookee there at them little Nozzies.

Heinies. Ain't that what they are, sure enough?"

I turned enough to see two men, in their sixties or so, dressed in chambray shirts and worn overalls — worn, but clean. One was tall and filled out, with red hair and glasses. The other was thicker and shorter, blond headed. I took them for Okies.

"Reckon you're right," said the shorter one. "Ol' Adolph's bosom buddies."

"What brings you boys to this part of town?" asked the tall guy, who looked pretty solid to boot, sizing up Elrich and the rest. A little muttering began in the assembled throng of onlookers. My ex-neighbor looked from the two old men to the rest of the crowd and then, with a quick nod of his head, said, "C'm'on," and walked away, trailed by the others.

Resisting the urge to shout something at their backs, I walked with Buster to the ticket booth, hearing as I left the two Okies wondering out loud, "How's come they wasn't goose-steppin'."

"How'd I do?" Buster asked.

"Tip top," I replied.

As I was digging in my pocket for a dime to give the granny in the booth, a middle-aged man with a thin face and round eyes stepped out in front of us. I'd noticed him standing in the movie house doorway as we were confronting the Bundists.

"Let these two in on me, Gertrude," he

said to the woman. And to us: "Enjoy the show, boys."

We both thanked him and went through, into the lobby, looking at one another.

"Manager, I guess," whispered Buster. "Think he's Jewish?"

"I wouldn't be surprised. At any rate, he's no Nazi lover," I whispered back. "But listen — we'd better watch ourselves. I know how these creeps work, and they could very well come after us, with or without rein-forcements, now that they know where we are."

"Should we leave?"

"What?" I said with a grin. "And miss riding with Tim McCoy _and_ the Three Mesquiteers? Plus, you know, I could be wrong."

He nodded, grinned back, and headed for the refreshment counter, where he dropped nearly a half-buck on candy bars, Milk Duds, Mary Janes, a Coke, and a bag of popcorn. I got my own popcorn and Coke, and we entered the dark interior, edging our way halfway down the side aisle while our eyes adjusted. On the screen, Betty Boop was teaching some Indians how to play swing music, and the kid audience was brimming over with commentary.

Picking a row about halfway up, we moved into it, doing our best to miss the toes of the youthful audience members in our row. A couple of them reacted negatively as we passed. There were two seats together right in the middle of the row — the best ones in the house, as far as I was concerned — and we settled in.

We'd no more than sat down when I heard a commotion behind us and felt my seventh sense start to tingle again. When I turned, I saw Elrich himself maneuvering down the aisle. He had a couple of others with him, including a big guy wearing a brown shirt instead of a white one, along with a Sam Browne belt. He didn't seem to be either of the two O.D. guys who'd tried to crack my skull that night in front of Mr. Gold, but there wasn't a hell of a lot of difference in their looks.

"Buster!" I whispered. "We've got company. Cover your face with your Coke cup."

Both of us buried our mugs in our drinks, pretending to guzzle them, watching the three Bundists out of the corners of our eyes.

When the gruesome group came to our row, they stopped and peered along the seats. By this time, a lot of the kid audience members had become aware of them, and as I watched over the top of my cup, the O.D. sort of flinched and picked something off his neck.

I almost gave us away by laughing. I think it was a Milk Dud, launched by an audience member.

Just about that time, the guy we took to be the manager showed up with a big flashlight, ordering them to leave. I didn't catch all of the interchange, but the Nazis were protesting that they'd bought their tickets and the manager was telling them they'd get a refund at the box office and that they were causing a disturbance. The word "cops" began cropping up. As the altercation got louder and more distracting, a chorus of boos and catcalls started to rise from the auditorium. By the time "The End" rolled on the Betty Boop cartoon, the theater guy had somehow managed to get them started back down the aisle toward the lobby. A few small missiles found their marks before the Bundists disappeared through the lobby doors.

I figured that would do it. I didn't think they'd seen us in the crowd and that they figured we'd just ducked out. So I let myself relax a little and turned my attention to the screen.

We happened to be in the building for the first chapter of a new Republic serial, which looks promising as hell. It's called <u>Dick Tracy's G-Men,</u> and while old Dick is once again played by Ralph Byrd, this time he's not a cop but a Federal, who runs up against a mastermind spy named Zaroff. (He's played by Irving Pichel from <u>Dracula's Daughter</u>, and the guy's pretty good.) It starts off with newsreel-type footage of Dick and his crew catching Zaroff, who ends up going to the gas chamber. But it turns out that Zaroff's not gassed at all; he got slipped some sort of drug that made it look like he was dead, but he really wasn't. And so, snatched away from the Reaper's scythe, he sets out to battle Tracy and the rest of our government boys.

I thought it was pretty swell, all things considered, and the kids loved it. They were pretty worked up by the time Tim McCoy's name popped up on the screen, cheering and carrying on. Lightning Bill, this time around, was unjustly accused of murder and, in an effort to clear himself, took on the name El Puma and guided an archeological expedition down in Mexico.

By the time the credits came up for the second feature, The Kansas Terrors, the Bund was pretty well gone from my mind. I guess it was a good picture, about a Caribbean island with a corrupt government, but I found myself thinking too much about Miss Gena Laubauch to stay up with the plot. I guess maybe it was because Jacqueline Wells was the female lead, and while she's a brunette and doesn't look a lot like Gena, there was something in her look and walk that put Gena front and center in my mind. I hoped she was doing all right with her folks back home, and then I realized that I was missing her. I know that sounds sappy, like something out of Love Story magazine, but it's the truth. I know that as long as Fehring is around she has to be away from Washington, but maybe things can change.

Naw, hell, I'm not in love or anything like that. Let's just say I'm intrigued. And that feeling's still with me, even if she's gone.

Anyway . . .

After The Kansas Terrors, the theater

showed a bunch of previews, mostly westerns and crime pictures, and we stayed and watched those, even as the kids began filing out. (I imagine this was the second time for the trailers to be shown.) So it was early evening by the time Buster and I got up to leave. The lobby was empty and darkened; I think they were closing for an hour or so to clean the auditorium for the nighttime crowd. Neither of us saw the manager on our way out. We pushed the door open, and just as we hit the sidewalk — along with a couple dozen kids who'd been in the audience with us — a yell went up: "There they are! Get 'em!"

The kids scattered like quail, leaving Buster and me standing there beside the ticket booth like a couple of statues. My seventh sense jangling, we threw open the door and sought the safety of the lobby. There's not much to admire with those Bund jackasses, but you have to say they show an inordinate amount of patience. I guess we'd been spotted after all when they'd bullied their way in, and there'd been a contingent of 'em waiting outside ever since.

Suddenly, the door slammed shut behind us. I looked to see the manager, quickly locking it.

"They must want you boys pretty badly," he said.

"Apparently," I told him. "You have a phone here?"

"In my office. C'm'on."

Leading us quickly behind the now-unmanned candy counter, he pushed aside a plush curtain to reveal a small space with a desk in the middle, covered with trade publications. I beat him to the Ameche, and, pushing aside a couple of <u>Boxoffice</u> magazines, picked up the receiver, dialed the operator, and asked her to connect me with the police. Once the connection went through, I asked for Sergeant Feinstein. In only moments that familiar gruff voice was on the line.

"Feinstein here. Who is this, and what do you want?"

"Sergeant, this is Robert Brown. You helped me the other day in front of Hy's Clothes for Men, and I'm calling you from the office of the Savoy Theater to tell you the Bund is after me again. They're waiting outside to catch my friend and me. Apparently, there's a price on my head. Do you suppose you could send someone by to run them off, sort of fly the flag, you know? Fire up the siren? I know that'd do the trick, and we'd sure appreciate it."

The silence at the other end went on far longer than I thought it should, as the seventh sense whipped like wind through me. Then, Feinstein said, angrily, "Shit, Brown. We aren't a bodyguard service. I'm working a murder right now and —"

"And," I interrupted, "you'll be working two more if you don't give us a hand. These Nazi bastards are out for blood. They're offering a hundred iron men to the one who puts me in the ground."

Again, a long pause.

"Aw, hell," he said finally, a little of the rancor leaving his voice. "Okay. I'll be right there. But this better be damned legitimate."

I was still assuring him it was when his end of the line clicked off. Turning to Buster, I said, "He's coming. Now, we have to time it just right." My gaze took in the manager as well. "We'll stay inside until the cops pull up, so we can draw those Nazis out into the open without getting our butts whipped in the process."

The manager nodded and we crept out into the lobby, just beside the door. He had his key out, waiting for my cue.

It seemed like we stood there for an eternity, but according to my strap watch, it was only about ten minutes before I heard the distant wail of a siren.

"Okay," I said. "Crack open that door."

He pushed it a little, until a thin shaft of electric light from the street shone through. At the same town, down the block, a shout: "Get ready! Someone's coming out!"

The siren noise intensified. As nearly as I could tell, it was just down the block. I peered out carefully. At this hour, there weren't as many pedestrians around as there had been, but there were still a few. I didn't want any of them to get hurt because of something I did.

Again, I knew the timing must be exactly right. And when it was, I said, "All right, Buster. Ready. Set. <u>Go</u>!"

Out we ran, banking on the notion that the police car would come roaring through just as we showed ourselves.

Except it wasn't a police car. It was an ambulance, and it sailed right past us.

We froze. In the darkness, I could see the figures of the Bundists, shadows popping up like mushrooms in the dark, heading our way. The sparse crowd between us and them seemed to dissolve, and the first wave hit before we could get back inside the theater; they slammed themselves against the door, trapping the manager inside, and then they turned on us.

Good place to end this letter, huh? Sorry, but I'm beat. You already know I wasn't killed. I'll give you the rest of it next time.

Your Republic-serial-like pal and faithful comrade,

Robert

October 22, 1939
Sunday night

Dear John,

I imagine you're getting sick to death of my cliffhangers, but after I write for a long while I just kind of hit a wall and have to do something else for a while. I don't have to tell you that the last letter I wrote goes on for a while. It took me maybe two hours this afternoon to write it, and I finally just ran out of gas.

Because I ran down, I cut it off in a place where I shouldn't have — right at the beginning of our tilt with the Bundists. My apologies, chum, but I just had to get out for a while and breathe some fresh air — as fresh as it gets in the City of Magnificent Intentions, anyway. So I put on my jacket and walked around outside in the impending dusk, meandering down the sidewalk past the houses and apartments that surround my boarding house, and trying not to think much about anything. As I wrote earlier, there's already a real snap in the air, even though it's only a week before Hallowe'en. I remember how sometimes it'd just be autumn one day and winter the next back in Minnesota. That's not the case here — it's more gradual — but I'll bet you it's going to be pretty cold pretty soon.

Then again, I don't imagine you're reading this to get a Washington weather report.

So, after my refreshing walk, I had one of Mrs. Dean's "cold suppers," cold cuts, bread, and milk, her standard fare on Sunday evenings. Thus fortified, I left my comrades — including Buster, who doesn't know I'm writing you about him — saying I was going to work on my book, and here I am, banging away at the typewriter keys again. I'm happy to say that all of my fellow residents, including Buster and Mrs. Dean, make a practice of not bothering me when they hear my old typer clacking away. That's good of 'em. Maybe they think I'm writing a future classic, and they can say they knew me when. Or maybe they're just being considerate.

Back to Saturday.

After the gaffe we made by thinking the cops were arriving, and acting accordingly, when it was actually the siren on an ambulance roaring through, Buster and I found ourselves in a bit of a pickle. There we were, surrounded by those beady-eyed little goose steppers, and me with a C-note price on my head. I don't have to tell you what my seventh sense was doing when I looked around at the crowd and gauged our odds.

Funny thing was, for a few moments, they seemed to be frozen as well, like the dog that finally catches the car and then doesn't

know what the hell to do next. We all just
sort of stood there, looking at one another,
a curious silence dropping over the scene.

Then, John, somewhere behind the threatening group, but not all that far away, I
heard an animalistic snarl that chilled my
blood and kicked the seventh sense into high
gear. There were no words, but it struck me
as nothing less than a bestial call to
action. I thought I'd heard it before, too —
or something a lot like it — during that wild
rainstorm on the roof of Woodward & Lothrop.

Suddenly, my Nazi ex-chum Elrich pushed
his way through the crowd, sap in hand, and
got close enough to take a swing at me,
shouting something in German. At least I
<u>think</u> it was in German. I didn't hear it all
that well because I was busy dodging the
first portentous swish of his blackjack, and
kicking out at him at the same time, the toe
of my shoe landing deep in a soft spot
between his legs. He folded like a poker
player with a seven-high hand.

The sudden movement seemed to galvanize
the crowd. All at once, the scene exploded,
and with shouted oaths, the Bundists moved as
one toward us, in a weird kind of slow
motion, a couple of them stopping to try and
pull Elrich to his feet. I heard his groans
and felt rather than saw Buster swing at the
Bundist who'd reached him first. He
connected, and it sounded like he'd hit a raw
side of beef.

In moments like that, it's funny what you do. As the seventh sense skittered through me like an explosion of spiders, I began counting in my mind the number of goose steppers we were facing. I'd gotten to 11 when I saw the glint of something unmistakable in the hand of one of them: a knife blade. And then, John, damned if another one didn't draw out an old long-barreled pistol.

My heart froze. These knuckleheads had <u>murder</u> on their feeble brains. The ones with weapons really wanted the reward on my head; <u>all</u> of 'em wanted me dead. And they'd cool Buster, too, for that matter, since he was with me.

Maybe it was the urging of the seventh sense that jolted me to action. Whatever it was, I grabbed Buster's shoulder, parrying off a blow with my right forearm, and shouted, "We've gotta haul ass. They're armed!" I could feel the crowd advancing on us.

Busy as he was peeling back the thumbs of a little guy who seemed hell-bent on strangling him, he managed to turn to me and pant out, "How do you figure to do that?"

I looked in front of me, where Elrich, held partially erect by a couple of his buddies, was shaking his head like a wounded bull. The sap he'd swung at me was still clutched in his hand.

"Like this!" I shouted, grabbing the blackjack out of his limp grasp and swinging it in a savage arc, back and forth. The guys propping Elrich up dropped him like a sack of cement and backed away from my swings. Buster pushed me along, and the two of us gathered speed as the Bundists jumped back to get out of the line of fire. I knew there was at least one knife and one pistol out there somewhere, and suddenly I wished I had thought to put on a protection spell before leaving my room. But then, I told myself, I've done so much talking that it wouldn't be working anyway.

So as we hightailed it away, I prayed instead, figuring each second that I'd be feeling the slash of a blade or the explosion of a bullet.

And then, my prayers were answered. As we went scurrying away from the Bundists, I heard the wail of a siren — and here came a cop car, roaring our way!

I hardly had time to appreciate it, though, as the bee-buzz of a bullet sailing past my ear cut through the siren's noise. Apparently, the little Nazi with the old pistol had recovered enough to take a potshot at us. Or maybe there was more than one firearm in that mob.

Behind me, another shot seemed to validate that last thought. It was followed by a loud curse. And then all hell broke loose, like the World War had started all over again. But we kept running. I didn't dare look back until we'd rounded the corner. Only then did Buster and I peer cautiously around the side of a building — at a scene that wouldn't have been out of place at the Battle of Verdun. Apparently, the one gun I'd seen in the assembled throng was just the tip of the iceberg. Now, they all seemed to be going off like firecrackers.

Which turned out to be a huge mistake for the Bundists. Because another car full of the fuzz had appeared behind Feinstein's vehicle, and those little Hitler lovers were now firing at the cops, who, using their autos as shields, returned their fire — almost casually, it seemed to me, although I knew that wasn't right. As I watched, a harness bull went down, grabbing his chest and dropping out of sight behind the second patrol wagon.

I knew the Bundists were dog meat now. As bad as it was to open fire on the police, actually shooting one was even worse, and a hail of concentrated gunfire followed from the vicinity of the autos. Two or three of the Bundists twirled and went down like they'd been poleaxed — one of them the O.D. officer I'd seen earlier inside the movie house.

Then, the shots tailed off, as quickly as they had started. Buster and I watched for another minute or two as the cops emerged from their cover and, guns drawn, advanced on a thoroughly beaten and frightened bunch of young Hitlerites. Those who weren't writhing — or motionless — on the sidewalk had their hands held high — "grabbing sky," as they say in the Westerns. Even as far away as we were, I could tell that some of them were shaking.

"Looks like we're safe now," I told Buster. "Let's go express our gratitude to the cavalry."

"Seems appropriate," he said.

So we stepped out from hiding — and almost got ourselves shot.

Maybe it was because the dusk made us seem to appear out of nowhere, but a couple of the officers whipped up their weapons when they saw us — figuring, maybe, we were part of the Bund. But then, thankfully, my old pal Sergeant Feinstein was there to shout, "Hold it!"

I gave him what I hoped was a jaunty wave. "Hi, Sergeant," I hollered.

We were about 100 feet away at that point, close enough to hear one of the other cops ask him, "You <u>know</u> these guys?"

Feinstein shook his head as though he were trying to clear it. "Yeah," he said. "<u>One</u> of 'em, anyway."

As we approached, I suddenly heard the same growling sound I'd heard just before we were attacked. It was carried by the wind from some point behind us, and while it might've been far away, it was nonetheless chilling. And I was pretty certain now that I knew its source.

Several of the little goose-steppers were laid out on the sidewalk, face-down and cuffed. A couple of them writhed, and I glimpsed a pool or two of blood. Then, a little ways away, my attention was drawn to a guy sprawled out across the pavement, bloodied and still. It was Elrich. Already, his body seemed bloated, unnatural. And even before one of the cops threw a blanket over his fresh corpse, I knew I'd seen him for the last time.

I couldn't help but stop and stare through the gloom for a moment as another harness bull walked up with the blanket. But it was only a moment. The harsh tones of Sergeant Feinstein broke my reverie.

"Damn your ass, Brown!" he muttered as I turned toward him. "You've done it now."

I looked at him, realizing, yeah, I guess it had been me who'd been responsible for all this. I was running that notion through my brain when, by golly, the sergeant actually grinned at me.

"Now," he said, "we've got grounds to round up every last one of these miserable little bastards." The smile left his face then, as he added, "You two gazabos get the hell out of here. This needs to be solely between the Bund and the cops." He made a sudden sweeping motion with his hand.

"Sure thing." I looked past him to the cop cars, where someone was putting a bandage on the downed cop's shoulder. "Your guy who got shot — is he going to be all right?"

"He'll live," returned Feinstein.

"So it's Cops one, Nazis zero," whispered Buster, but not so quietly that Feinstein couldn't hear it. The sergeant shook his head slowly. "Yeah. Ask your buddy about the stiff. But do it away from here." When we didn't immediately jump, he added, more loudly, "Go on, dammit! We're already starting to draw a crowd."

We exited, and I tried not to look at Elrich as we passed, heading back the way we'd come. People passed us in the deepening dusk, eyes wide, headed for the scene of the gun battle. I heard the far-off wail of sirens on another couple of squad cars, and just when we'd put several yards of sidewalk between ourselves and the captured and wounded Bundsmen, I caught Feinstein's booming voice again. Turning my head as we walked on, I could barely make out the figure of the theater manager, under the marquee lights, cowering a bit as Feinstein's voice cut through the dusk: "*You* called us! Get it? Forget those two jerks. They were never here!"

"Wonder where we were, then?" asked Buster, grinning at me. His teeth shone whitely in the near-dark.

"Just minding our own business, I guess," I told him. "Enjoying a couple of shoot-'em-ups at the local Bijou."

"That sergeant back there — he's the cop who brought you to the boarding house that first night you were with us, isn't it? After you'd had that fight with, well, pretty much those same guys that just tried to mess us up?"

"Right."

"I _thought_ I recognized him. I just saw him in the doorway for a few seconds, but I don't forget faces."

"You'd make a hell of a detective, Buster," I said, and he straightened a bit as we walked. I think it was out of pride.

"Yeah. He said to ask you about the dead guy, too."

I didn't say anything for a moment, maybe because I didn't know exactly what _to_ say. Then, I told him, "He's the one who got me into the Bund in the first place; my next door neighbor at the apartment I had when I first moved to town. We had a couple of scraps. I signed a complaint against him, and he spent a little time in the cooler because of it. He was a weasel, but that doesn't mean I'm happy he's dead."

We were lucky. Just as we turned the corner, a streetcar arrived, going in the direction we wanted. Funny enough, just after we got on, we heard the noise of a couple of people clambering up behind us, but when we turned and locked eyes with them they hauled ass like a turpentined cat.

"Bundists," I said to Buster.

"Uh-huh. Look at 'em go. They may not stop until they get to Berlin."

He laughed, and I did too.

We did a lot of laughing between there and the boarding house, going over our adventure. Every once in a while, I'd get a twinge of — what? — <u>regret</u>, maybe, when I thought of Elrich lying on the cold sidewalk under that blanket, gone forever. At those times, the laughter would die in me. But then, Buster would recall something like how some kid hit the O.D. with a Milk Dud, and we'd be off again.

It went like that until we jumped down from the street car at our stop. As soon as our feet hit the pavement, a faint buzz from my private warning system ping-ponged through me, kind of like that far-off artillery fire you hear in the background when Edward R. or one of the other Murrow Boys do their short-wave broadcasts from a European battlefield.

I stopped and turned to Buster.

"Why don't you go on in? I'll be with you in a minute," I said.

His brows knitted and he started to say something but thought better of it. I think he liked the idea of being the one who'd break the news about our adventure to our fellow boarders. So he headed for the front door, and I slipped around back, trying to follow what I thought my seventh sense was telling me.

I had just rounded the corner of the boarding house when I slammed on my brakes.

There, standing at the foot of the stairs to Mr. Saki's garage apartment was both Mr. Saki and the Mountain Witch! I suppose it was to avoid being spotted by a bystander out in the street, but for whatever reason she'd taken the form of the middle-aged Asian lady that she'd used to visit me. I knew who she was; in my mind's eye, I _saw_ her for what she was. Or perhaps she just let her guard down for a moment when she saw who I was.

At the same time, I looked above them to the roof of Mr. Saki's apartment, and I glimpsed two or three of those hideous monkeys that had looked in on me earlier. They seemed to be watching Mr. Saki and the Yamamba. Then, in a twinkling, they were gone, so quickly that I wasn't sure I'd actually seen them at all.

I looked back toward the two, nodded and smiled, and they nodded back. This didn't seem to be a good time to stop and chat, and they didn't seem so inclined, so I hurried past them and up the back stairs to the bathroom, where I threw some water on my face, took a couple of deep breaths, and headed downstairs. The skittering of the seventh sense still ran through me, but it was at a simmer, not a boil.

Clyde, Nick, and Mrs. Dean were together at the table, sharing another of her cold suppers, when I reached the bottom of the stairs, and I could hear and see that Buster was going full throttle, enjoying the attention he was getting. The thought occurred to me that he was doing exactly what Sergeant Feinstein didn't want us to do — that is, to put ourselves in the picture as the instigators. But since he wasn't there, I didn't see any harm in it.

"__There's__ the other local hero," said a grinning Nick when I entered the dining room. "C'm'on over, Nazi fighter, and give us the low down. Did Buster here really save your bacon like he says he did?"

Buster flushed to the roots of his blond hair, and Clyde and Nick laughed. Even Mrs. Dean cracked a smile.

"Now __wait__ a minute, you guys," Buster began. "I never said —"

"Shhhh," interrupted Mrs. Dean. "Listen."

She nodded toward the big radio, which had been playing dance music. A news announcer had broken in to tell all about the "deadly" encounter between the D.C. cops and the German American Bund. According to the announcer, members of that group had tried to kill a police officer who'd been engaged in breaking up one of their "violent demonstrations."

Buster and I grinned at each other, even as the sight of Elrich and the others on the sidewalk flashed through my mind. But then, as I reached for bread and some roast beef, the warning bells increased their ringing inside me, and I heard the sound of a car door slamming in front of the house.

Our grins faded, and the room grew quiet as we all listened to the sound of two people's footsteps, clacking up the front walk, one set lighter and quicker than the other. Then, a peaked hat appeared in the glass of the doorway.

"Oh, hell," Buster said softly. "More cops."

I shook my head quickly to silence him. We didn't need to alarm anyone, especially our fellow boarders — and our landlady.

All eyes were on the doorway when the knock came. Mrs. Dean started toward the door, but Nick put his arm out.

"I'll go," he said. Maybe he felt he needed to do that because he was the oldest of us boarders, or because of some sense of gallantry, but whatever the reason he strode to the door and opened it.

And there on the porch, accompanied by a hackie in a peaked cap that looked like something worn by harness bulls, stood Gena.

Looking over Nick's shoulder to where Mrs. Dean stood, she said, "You're Mrs. Dean, aren't you?"

Our landlady nodded, a bit dumbfounded.

Gena's eyes flicked to mine. "Robert's told me about you. You've talked to me on the phone, too. I'm Gena."

For a moment, no one said anything, even

the cabbie, who was carrying a couple of suitcases.

"Oh," said Mrs. Dean finally. "Yes. I'm sorry, Gena. Please come in."

She stepped through the threshold, giving us all a ten-thousand-watt smile. "Thank you," she said. "Might I have a room for the night? It's been a long trip for me and I'm very tired. I'll certainly be happy to pay you."

Again, silence. The guys looked at one another, probably thinking what I was thinking: Mrs. Dean, as far as we knew, had never taken in a female boarder.

It was Mrs. Dean who spoke first.

"Well, certainly," she said. "If you don't mind sharing a room with me."

Gena shook her head. "Not at all. I'm grateful." Then, walking to me, taking my arm, and still wearing that smile, she asked, "So what's the emergency?"

I was stunned. When I didn't answer immediately, she continued, frowning.

"You look like you don't understand what I'm saying. You're the one who asked me to come. You said it was very important. Why, you even sent me train fare from Milwaukee."

"Gena, I don't know what you're talking about."

"Are you saying it was someone else who did all of that — wrote me the telegram, sent me the money, saying it was you?"

"I —"

She seemed to wobble then, and Nick helped her to one of Mrs. Dean's big antimacassared chairs. As she sat down and pulled a handkerchief from her purse, I paid off the cab driver, giving him a good tip, and hauled the suitcases off the porch. The other guys, Buster included, milled around, not quite knowing what they should do.

"Could one of you gentlemen take Gena's bags to my room?" asked Mrs. Dean. "There's a trundle bed there she can use."

The gallant Nick was the first to respond, and he disappeared quickly with the bags. Gena, meanwhile, reclined in the big, over-stuffed chair, looking lost. Mrs. Dean stood beside her.

"Mrs. Dean," I said softly, "may Gena and I have a few private words?"

She looked at Gena, and then at me. "Not upstairs," she said primly. "That's for you men only."

"I know," I returned. "Maybe the kitchen."

She nodded. We passed Nick on the way and shut the door behind us.

"Robert," she almost whispered. "I'm sorry for giving you that line. I know you didn't send for me. But I know who did."

She'd carried her purse with her, and suddenly I was looking down the muzzle of a loaded .38 snub nose revolver.

"And I've come to kill that shaggy-haired

son-of-a-bitch!" she said, trying to keep her voice from rising.

You know what, John? I wouldn't be at all surprised if she did.

Your pal and faithful comrade,
    Robert

ACKNOWLEDGMENTS

First of all, big thanks to Bill and Lara Bernhardt for their kindnesses toward us and their shepherding of this story from manuscript to publication. Any success that we see with this book should rightfully be shared with them.

Also, much gratitude to Hattie Brown and Kimberlee Brown-Boyer for allowing new stories to continue to see print after Robert's passing; to my media team, Lourdes Alcala, Joey Hambrick, and No. 2 son Steven Wooley for all their help and advice; and No. 1 son Jonathan for the wonderfully evocative cover designs on this and the reissued Cleansing books.

Finally, Robert and I were encouraged by a number of friends and fans, including, but certainly not limited to (in alphabetical order), Carole Bender, Chad Calkin, John Hamill, Bruce Hershenson, Mark Hickman, John Locke, John McMahan, Phil Nelson, Michael H. Price, Buddy Saunders, Ron Wolfe, and Mark S. Wooley.

Thanks to all of you; you made this one possible.

— JW

ABOUT THE AUTHORS

Robert A. Brown spent most of his working life in public education, seeing duty as both a reading specialist and administrator in the Oklahoma City public school system. During that time, he also authored and sold several nonfiction pieces dealing with the Great Depression and its popular culture, including Western movies and the so-called "Spicy" magazines of the period. During the trading-card boom of the 1990s, for instance, Brown supplied the art and text for two sets of pulp-magazine-related cards for Kitchen Sink Press, both of which are now collector's items.

Internationally known as a collector of movie paper, pulps, old radio shows, and other pop-culture memorabilia, Robert was a founder of the Oklahoma Alliance of Fans (OAF), a group of collectors with interests in nostalgia and collecting; he edited, published, and wrote for several issues of that fraternal group's newsletter. Some 20 years ago, he began writing letters, typed on authentic period stationery, to OAF co-founder John Wooley, using his deep knowledge of the 1930s to portray himself as a WPA employee beset by rural horrors. Wooley, who'd been writing professionally since 1979, recognized immediately that his old friend was onto something, and those letters became the basis of Babylon Books' three-volume series The Cleansing.

The success of those novels led to another Brown-Wooley

collaboration, and the two were making inroads into the second book of the Demons in D.C. series on January 13, 2025, when a myriad of health issues finally brought Robert down.

This book is the last one to be completed before his death. The second and concluding volume is due out in late 2025.

John Wooley made his first professional sale in the late 1960s, placing a script with the legendary *Eerie* magazine. He's now in his sixth decade as a professional writer, having written three horror novels with co-author Ron Wolfe, including *Death's Door*, which was one of the first books released under Dell's Abyss imprint and was also nominated for a Bram Stoker Award. His solo horror and fantasy novels include *Awash in the Blood*, *Ghost Band*, and *Dark Within*, the latter a finalist for the Oklahoma Book Award.

Wooley is also the author of the critically acclaimed biographies *Wes Craven: A Man and His Nightmares* and *Right Down the Middle: The Ralph Terry Story*. He has co-written or contributed to several volumes of Michael H. Price's Forgotten Horrors series of movie books and co-hosts the podcast of the same name. His other writing credits include the 1990 TV film *Dan Turner, Hollywood Detective* and several documentaries, notably the Learning Channel's *Hauntings Across America*. Among the comics and graphic novels he's scripted are *Plan Nine from Outer Space*, the authorized version of the alternative-movie classic, as well as the recent collections *The Twilight Avenger* and *The Miracle Squad*.